# Get What You Give

Also by Stephanie Perry Moore

Perry Skky Jr. series

*Prime Choice*
*Pressing Hard*
*Problem Solved*
*Prayed Up*
*Promise Kept*

Beta Gamma Pi series

*Work What You Got*
*The Way We Roll*
*Act Like You Know*
*Got It Going On*

# Get What You Give

## A Beta Gamma Pi Novel
## Book 5

## Stephanie Perry Moore

KENSINGTON PUBLISHING CORP.

www.kensingtonbooks.com

DAFINA BOOKS are published by

Kensington Publishing Corp.
119 West 40th Street
New York, NY 10018

ISBN-13: 978-0-7582-3446-9
ISBN-10: 0-7582-3446-5

First Trade Paperback Printing: May 2010
10  9  8  7  6  5  4  3  2

Printed in the United States of America

For
*Angela Graham*
*&*
*Shirley Kimbro*

*(ladies in my sorority)*

*Being in a group with strong women isn't always easy.
Confrontations happen when people are passionate
about their views. As I reflect back, I've learned so much
that I placed in this novel. I pray it helps others learn
the best ways to get along. May God bless you and
yours and every reader of this book and series.*

# ACKNOWLEDGMENTS

Though I love my sorority with all my heart, sometimes it does not bring joy. There's a ton of work that has to be done, and I don't have that much time to do it. There are many people to interact with, and, try as I might, I do not have a chance to get to everyone. And no matter how well the intentions or how great the planning, I can't please everyone. Coming up short on so much is frustrating. So I fall to my knees—before meetings, during meetings, and after meetings—for direction. God has helped me see that as long as I give much and keep being willing to better my mistakes, I will do the sorority more good than harm, and I will enjoy it more and more each day.

Penning a series on a made-up sorority was an eye opener for me. It's hard looking at yourself and asking the tough questions. Why do you strive for leadership in the sorority? Why do you feel people should love you as a sister? When you didn't reach your highest educational goals, why do you feel you can tell others not to falter in that area? When you didn't walk with Christ daily in college, how can you show others the way? Why is public service so important to you, really? Whew, so many questions, never the perfect answers. I guess I learned as I delved into these five books that the sorority experience is what you make of it. And the titles say it best. You may not be the best leader, but work what you got. You may not always get along with your sorors, but the way you roll is together. You may not be the wisest yet, but act like you know you're worthy to learn more each day. You may not deserve God's love, or anyone else's, but know, because of His grace, you've got it going on, and you have a forgiving heart. You may outgrow people and circumstances, but keep giving them more than they give you, and you'll always be able to sleep well. God loves you, and society needs you to serve. As the late, great Michael Jackson taught us, we must all work to make this world a better place. Here is a big hug of thanks to everyone who helps me keep giving:

To my family: parents, Dr. Franklin and Shirley Perry, Sr.; brother, Dennis, and sister-in-law, Leslie; my mother-in-law, Ms. Ann; and extended family Rev. Walter and Marjorie Kimbrough, Bobby and Sarah Lundy, Antonio and Gloria London, Cedric and Nicole Smith, Harry and Nino Colon, Brett and Loni Perriman, Donald and Deborah Bradley, and Paul and Tammy Garnes—your love helps me give more. Don't stop loving hard. I'm more concerned about the world because of your support.

To my publisher, Kensington / Dafina Books: Your knowledge of what works in publishing keeps my books moving. Don't stop believing in YA books. I'm a more successful author because of my association with you. Also, special thanks to my copy editor, Hillary Campbell, for her work on the Beta Gamma Pi series.

To my writing team: Beverly Smith, Cynthia Boyd, Deborah Thomas, Ciara Roundtree, Chantel Morgan, Carolyn O'Hora, Ashley Morgan, Alyx Pinkston, Jenell Clark, Cassandra Brown, Dorcas Washington, Vanessa Davis Griggs, Victoria Christopher Murray, Sonya Jenkins, Edythe Woodruff, Beverly Jenkins, Chandra Dixon, Bridget Fielder, and Myra Brown Lee—your truthfulness helps me keep the pages real. Don't stop prereading my work. I'm better at what I do because of your input.

To my sorority sisters of Delta Sigma Theta Sorority, Inc., particularly the National President, Cynthia Butler-McIntyre; Southern Regional Director, Christine Nixon; the National Society of Arts and Letters; and the Southern Regional Membership Services Committee—your inclusion of me strengthens my work ethic. Don't stop making a difference in the community. I'm living a fuller life as I serve with you.

To my emergent children: Dustyn Leon, Sydni Derek, and Sheldyn Ashli—your growth makes me thankful for each day. Don't stop trying. I'm hoping you strive to please God.

To my hubby, Derrick C. Moore—your desire to give young people your all is contagious. Don't stop being you, and remember Jillian needs you. I'm happy being your partner.

To my readers—your time and trust means a ton to me. Don't stop being open to the blessing a book can bring. I'm so thankful you have gotten this book.

And to my God—Your strength You give me to endure the tough times is a blessing. Don't stop giving me ideas to share with the world. I'm trying hard to bless them.

# BETA GAMMA PI
## TRADITIONS, CUSTOMS, & RITES

### Founding Data

Beta Gamma Pi was founded in 1919 on the campus of Western Smith College by five extraordinary women of character and virtue.

### Sorority Colors

Sunrise lavender and sunset turquoise are the official colors of Beta Gamma Pi. The colors symbolize the beginning and the end of the swiftly passing day and remind each member to make the most of every moment.

### Sorority Pin

Designed in 1919, the pin is made of the Greek letters Beta, Gamma, and Pi. This sterling silver pin is to be worn over the heart on the outermost garment. There are five stones in the Gamma: a ruby representing courageous leadership, a pink tourmaline representing genuine sisterhood, an emerald representing a profound education, a purple amethyst representing deep spirituality, and a blue sapphire representing unending service.

Anytime the pin is worn, members should conduct themselves with dignity and honor.

# The B Pin

The B Pin was designed in 1920 by the founders. This basic silver pin in the shape of the letter B symbolizes the beginning step in the membership process. The straight side signifies character. The two curves mean yielding to God and yielding to others. It is given at the Pi Induction Ceremony.

# Sorority Flower

The lily is the sorority flower and it denotes the endurance and strength the member will need to be a part of Beta Gamma Pi for a lifetime.

# Sorority Stone

The diamond is the sorority stone which embodies the precious and pure heart needed to be a productive member of Beta Gamma Pi.

# Sorority Call

Bee-goh-p

# Sorority Symbol

The eagle is the symbol of Beta Gamma Pi. It reflects the soaring greatness each member is destined to reach.

# Sorority Motto

A sisterhood committed to making the world greater.

# The Pi Symbol

The Bee insect is the symbol of the Pi pledges. This symbolizes the soaring tenacity one must possess to become a full member of Beta Gamma Pi.

# Contents

# Get What You Give

# BABBLE

"Would you risk your own life to possibly try to save someone else's? People talk about best friends, including you, Hailey Grant, but would you really lay it all on the line to make sure your best friend was spared from pain?" my roommate, Teddi Spencer, asked as I tried to study. "I mean, 'cause you're not acting like it."

What was she talking about? We were tighter than tight, and she knew I had her back. But every now and then when I wasn't doing something she agreed with, she'd try to lay a guilt trip on me. So I kept studying and ignored her tail, hoping she'd get the picture and leave me alone.

Actually, most folks who knew us all last year wondered how we remained friends. We were pretty different. I was about facts, and she was about fiction. There was nothing wrong with dreaming, but you had to get your head out of the clouds to actually get things done. I swear, her address was La-La Land. She knew how to get to me, but I knew I could never intentionally walk out of her life. Teddi had lost more in her high school years than my heart could bear. If our friendship made her happy and brought her joy, I'd do anything to protect that.

"I'm just saying. I gotta win the election, Hailey. And you're not helping. That Covin Randall guy thinks just because he's the state senator's son, everybody's on his jock. Well, I'm . . ." Teddi continued her rant about her disgust for her rival SGA opponent in the upcoming election as I tuned her out.

I looked at my short, frail, light-skinned friend. She had been through so much over the past two years I'd known her. We were now sophomores at Western Smith College. When she'd lost her parents in a tragic car accident her senior year, she'd moved in with her grandmother and begun attending my high school.

She hadn't known anybody, and she'd seemed like she was in deep pain. I had taken it upon myself to help and befriend her. I didn't know where that had come from— you know, the knack to want to help someone out. I guess somewhere deep inside me there was a place that felt I should give back since I'd been taken care of all my life. I had two great parents. My uncle, Wade Webb, was the president of the college I attended, for goodness' sake. My older sister, Hayden, had gone here, and everyone remembered what a gem she was. Honestly, I wasn't a princess, but I hadn't had any tragedies in my life either. Because I've had great experiences and supportive people in my life, I guess I felt the need to help those who had no one.

Teddi sat on my bed next to me in our dorm room and turned my face toward her. "You're not even listening to me, Hailey. I mean, I need to win this election. The last president we had was a disgrace. The students at Western Smith need to feel confident in their new president, and, personally, I don't think that right now anyone who uses the bathroom standing up qualifies enough to win the confidence of the entire student body. We need a gender change."

"What are you saying, Teddi? We need a female president?" I asked, thinking she needed more reasons than that to feel she should win over her opponent.

She got a little loud with me and said, "You got a problem with that? You don't think I'm strong enough, do you? You don't think I can lead? I mean, why would any of us females around here trust someone who leads by what's between their legs?"

"No, no. I'm just saying just because one male was stupid doesn't mean the others have to be the same," I jumped up and said, calmly defending myself.

Teddi paced back and forth and started freaking out. "Well, I'm just saying we need a change, and you're completely not behind me. You're supposed to be my campaign manager, and you're not even on my side."

"Why are you overexaggerating the issue?" I asked. "I'm just telling you how I feel."

"Because we need to come up with a strategy. I've seen posters all over campus for this guy, and my posters aren't even up yet. Isn't that your job?" Teddy asked me pointedly.

Quickly, I reminded her she was the reason we hadn't

gotten a lot accomplished with her campaign. "Listen, chick, I love you, but you're full of it. Every idea I've had, you shot down. It's your fault you don't have a platform. I drill you on basic questions, like why do you want to be the Student Government Association President, and you stutter and say because we don't need a male. That's bull. I can't put out material on your campaign when you have no legit ideas. So don't try to blame this on me."

Teddi sank to her bed. "Then say I'm just a loser and just quit my campaign. Don't help me."

"Oh, girl, don't be melodramatic. I know your butt. You have substance. Find it and let's get a plan. I've seen the posters from the other candidate. People in the dorm have been hovering all around them. But we can get yours out—there's still time," I said. I wasn't planning to bail on her, but we did need to get cracking if she wanted to win.

She sat up, clung to me, and became paranoid. "Were the guys all into his poster? The chauvanists. See—they stick together. We gotta do the same, Hailey, I'm telling you. Now I'm actually thinking that living in a coed dorm was not a good choice. How am I going to get support from the girls *and* the guys?"

"We can do it, Teddi. But with all these fine brothers I've been seeing coming in and out of here . . . this is completely a good choice. It took hell and high water to convince my mom to agree to it," I said, knowing how overprotective my mom was since she'd let Hayden live off campus in an apartment four years back and worried about boys having too much access.

It had taken a lot to make my mom ease up. I was in

college, and there was no getting around me interacting with guys. At least I would be supervised in a dorm that had males on the other side of the building. Also, once my mom had met Teddi, she'd relaxed. Teddi wasn't boy crazy, and she wasn't going to let me run wild either.

"Do you smell that?" I said to her as I got a whiff of something really strong.

Suddenly, I knew I was not imagining the smell as smoke seeped in through the bottom of the door. The smoke was making it hard to breathe. I became uneasy. What was going on?

"No, I don't smell anything, Hailey. I'm trying to talk to you, but your focus is on everything else in the world. You're not being my best friend or my campaign manager right now. You're talking about all the reasons I don't have a shot. I'll listen to your platform ideas. Give them to me again."

Covering my mouth so as not to inhale whatever was seeping through the door, I said, "Great—Teddi, we can work on it later. But now something is seriously wrong. Look at the door."

As I moved to the door to find out what was up, someone knocked loudly from the other side. "Are y'all in there? Open up! Open up!"

"It's probably nothing, Hailey. Relax," Teddi said.

She was clueless. As I walked to the door I tossed her a towel to cover her mouth with, but she threw it back at me. A gray fog was filling the air. She needed to quit tripping. There had to be something burning. I walked over to the door and answered it.

A cute girl wearing a Beta Gamma Pi shirt—who looked

familiar—was at the door. "Hey, we gotta get out. There's a fire. We've got to move quickly," she said calmly but with urgency.

Teddi didn't hear what she said. All she was focused on was the girl's shirt as Teddi walked to the door. "I knew you looked familiar. Cassidy Cross—cool. I didn't know you lived in our building. You were on the last Beta line. BGP, the sorority for me."

"Yeah cool, but like I was telling your roommate, we gotta go. There's a fire!"

I tried to stay calm, but upon hearing the news, Teddi couldn't hold herself together. "Oh, my gosh! A fire! What about my things—your things, Hailey? What about my parents' box? It's the only thing I have left of them."

As more smoke filled the doorway, I couldn't let her continue to ramble, so I grabbed her arm and said, "We can't think about that now, Teddi. We have to get out of here! We need to get out of this building, and quick."

The smoldering cloud in the hallway almost made it difficult to breathe. I instantly started coughing. I shook my head to stay focused. I knew I had to get out of the building, but when I looked behind me, Teddi was still at our doorway. If I had to, I would pull her outside myself because she wasn't moving.

"Hailey, I have to get my stuff. My jewelry. My mom's picture. My dad's Bible. That stuff is important. I have to go get the box. Hailey, don't you understand?"

To a rational person, that made no sense. The only thing we needed to be worried about was getting our tails out of there. However, I knew all the pain she had been through, and I didn't want to add more, so I decided to help Teddi get her things. Because Teddi's parents were gone, this stuff was all she had of them.

"Okay, tell me what you want me to grab. Where is your little trunk?" I said, referring to the silver box in which she stored everything.

"It's under my bed, but it's all the way over there. I can't—I can't breathe, Hailey." Teddi clutched her heart.

"What are y'all doing? I said y'all have to get out of here!" Cassidy said as she came back to our room. She had gone knocking on other people's doors. "Y'all have to get out of here." Her mouth was covered, but we could understand what she was saying.

"Go ahead, Teddi. I'll get your box."

"Thank you," she said, crying hysterically. "Thank you, Hailey. How . . . how could I have doubted your love for me?"

The dorm beds were so heavy I needed to think about how I was quickly going to get in and get out. When my mom had come up a week ago, it had taken four of us to move the beds. *How am I going to move these by myself now?* I thought to myself. *Come on, Hailey. Think.* Then I figured it out. I could fit under the bed; I would just slide under and grab her box.

But I was becoming more and more tired. I wasn't a geek, but I knew the smoke was wearing down on my heart. With as little as I had in me, I decided to give it one last try. She needed the box.

That was all I could muster. I knew Teddi would never

forgive herself if I risked my life for her personal belongings. I didn't pray often, but at this moment I could use a prayer. So I thought, *Lord, I know I've been a little angry at You for taking my friend's parents. I guess if You wouldn't have, she wouldn't be in my life. Out of lemons we're supposed to make lemonade, right? Help me get it, because I need to get out of here.*

I grunted and got the box, exited the room, and went out into the hallway. I could barely see, but I knew which way the stairs were. When I got there, there was more moaning. Screams were filling the clouded air.

Cassidy said to me, "The door is jammed. We can't get out. And your friend, Teddi—look!"

When I looked down, I saw that Teddi had passed out. This moment was so terrifying there weren't any words to describe it. At this moment the smoke got denser, and I couldn't even see down to the other end of the hallway. I knew we were through.

"Help! Help! Oh, my gosh, help!" I screamed out, joining Cassidy and other people from our floor in their cries for help.

I just started praying to God to help us. *I know I don't come to You often, Lord. But I do care, and I love You.*

I was going on and on until Cassidy shook me. "Come on, don't give up. Help us yell for help!"

As we continued yelling, the door we were banging on finally sprang open. Two guys from upstairs who had been heading out had stopped to help us. The air coming in was fresh and couldn't have come at a better time.

This guy shouted, "We heard y'all! There was a beam blocking the door! We gotta get out of here! Look at the fire! Help them, Jake!"

The Jake guy motioned for the other two girls to leave, and they fled fast. "Come on!"

Cassidy and I pulled Teddi to the stairs, and the other guy slammed the steel door shut behind us to momentarily hold the fire. Cassidy and I tried to move my roommate. Her limp body was not responsive.

"Cassidy, go!" I shouted. "I got her!"

"I'm not leaving you guys. You need my help," Cassidy said as the smoke started to seep under the steel door.

"Run, girl—I'll help them," the stranger said as he shoved Cassidy down the first step.

I looked closely at the guy who was risking his life. He could've kept going, but he'd decided to stop to help us. The smoke made my vision blurry, and it was like I knew him, but I didn't know him. I was thankful he cared enough to help.

"Is this Teddi?" he asked as he looked at her face.

"Yes," I confirmed as we both tried to lift her. "You know her?"

"Oh, I gotta help her out of here. They will think I threw the election on purpose," he uttered as he nodded.

As we got Teddi off the ground, his last comment made me know where I knew him from . . . the posters! This was Covin Randall. He was Teddi's opponent.

When his eyes met mine, I buckled a little. "I can't lift her. She's too heavy."

"You're weak now. And you need to save your strength to get out of here. I got her. You go ahead," he said to me, and I headed down.

The fire was spreading. It was rumbling, almost talking. Safety was just one flight down, but it felt endless.

As soon as I got outside, a fireman met me. "Miss, are you the last one?"

"No, I know there are two people left. My roommate passed out. Somebody's bringing her. Please go help them."

He called out to another firefighter, and I was swooped into someone's arms and taken to safety.

As the fresh air from outside hit me, I felt like my lungs were screaming for joy. My uncle rushed to my aid, and the firefighter placed me in his arms and gave him instructions to take me to the ambulance for evaluation.

He hugged me tight, repeatedly saying, "I thought you were gone. I thought you couldn't get out. My sister would never have forgiven me if something had happened to you on my watch. I thank God."

"Sir, we need to check her out and give her some oxygen," one of the EMS workers said when he would not let me go.

I kept watching the door. I spotted Cassidy and Jake. Thankfully, they were all right. Then I squinted my eyes as I honed in on Cassidy clutching her hands together like life was not grand. Covin and Teddi hadn't come out yet. I refused treatment and ran closer to the door. As the tears rolled down my face, I wondered what was happening inside. I prayed, *Lord, You helped me out. Please, though, please help them out, too.*

Finally, a firefighter had Teddi in his arms. I was relieved. Then the next second, when I didn't see Covin, I was terrified again. He'd saved us, so he had to be saved. Why was he nowhere in sight?

"Where is the guy? I'm certain there was someone else in there!" I screamed, trying to go back myself.

Jake yelled, "She's right! My boy Covin is in there!"

"Yes, he told me to get out of there. You have to get him!" Cassidy cried out, finally breaking down because of the grave circumstances she knew Covin was facing.

I darted to the blazing door.

"Another firefighter is on his way in to get him—the smoke was too much. Covin was behind me when I took the girl, but then he tripped over the debris," the firefighter said, holding me back from going in. "It's okay, miss. We're gonna get him out."

The EMS worker with Teddi yelled for assistance. "I need help over here—she's unresponsive!"

My uncle rushed over to her. My heart felt like it should be in the Olympics, as fast as it was racing. I had been so happy to see Teddi, I'd forgotten she'd been out of it for at least ten minutes before she was pulled from the building. And as I turned back to the dorm, more of it was in flames, and Covin was not out.

"Oh, my gosh, this is horrible. This is bad. They have to be okay," I said between my own coughs.

Another EMS worker came over to me, practically forcing the mask on my face, and said, "I got to be blunt. Breathe into this before you fall over, and we have to cart you away. Hush up. Right now is no time to babble."

## GRATITUDE

*A*fter taking three deep breaths, I handed the mask to the paramedic and said, "I gotta make sure everyone else is okay. Please trust me, I'm fine."

My eyes were watering as I looked at the paramedic. My best friend was laid out on a cot with EMTs working overtime to make sure she was okay. The guy who'd saved me was not even out of the building. How could I concentrate on me? I had to be there for them.

The paramedic glared back at me. I think he saw I was seriously concerned for the others. He eased up a bit and said, "Okay, okay. Take a few more intakes of oxygen. Let me check your vitals, and then I can release you. I don't mean to sound insensitive, but you can't do anyone any good if you're ill."

Looking at his badge, I saw his last name was Grayson.

Mr. Grayson, who seemed like he never smiled, had a point. Though I hated taking care of myself, after I breathed more into the mask, I felt ten times better.

When he gave me the all-clear, he proved me wrong and grinned just a tad. "I'm glad you're okay."

I thanked him and then rushed over to Teddi's side. I couldn't get that close because they were putting her in the ambulance. I hugged my uncle tight.

He gave me a semi-positive update. "They did get her stable. They're just making sure she's completely out of the woods. You need to go sit and rest. Your mom should be here any minute."

When I saw Teddi sitting up, I exhaled. Then I was distracted by the commotion coming from near the building. I had been too busy talking to my uncle and getting oxygen to see what had happened. But the building was completely down on one side. People were beside themselves. Uncle Wade started walking toward the bigger group, and I followed. He could not keep me away.

"That Covin guy saved my life," I argued when my uncle gave me the mean look to sit down. "I've got to make certain he's okay."

My uncle stopped walking, and with an impressed stare said, "Covin Randall made sure you were out?" I nodded. "He's a super guy. Was on the SGA the last two years. Just another reason I know he's got the character to make a great class president."

Before I could tell my uncle I agreed and that I would probably be letting my best friend down with my new revelation of who'd get my vote, Cassidy dashed up to us. She was out of breath, and I held mine. Would Covin even be around to run for the election?

"The guy is okay," Cassidy said, hugging me. "The firefighter got him out just in time."

I hugged her back so tightly. I was overjoyed that this guy I didn't know, but felt connected to, was okay. I quickly went through the crowd to see Covin myself. I had to thank him. I had to hug him. I had to see for myself that he was okay.

Covin was coughing excessively. So much so, it was scary. The paramedics called for everyone to back up. He fell onto the gurney. When others moved back, I kept walking toward him.

When I finally got to his ear, I uttered, "Thank you so much. You saved me. You saved my friend. You were so courageous. Thanks for being our hero."

Mr. Grayson, my EMS worker friend, came over and said, "Ma'am, we have to make sure you all are okay and get you away from this building. You will have time later to thank him. Let us make sure y'all are safe by getting back. Plus, we need to check your friend out."

I looked down at Covin, and he really was out of it. Probably hadn't heard anything I'd said. He was covered in smut and soot. He yelled out in pain when they touched his leg. The EMS guys said he was probably burned. I knew I had to get back and let them do their work.

"Oh, my gosh! Hailey! You're okay!" my mom screamed as she rocked me back and forth, getting my mind off feeling useless.

My head was pounding a little, and though I had been

cleared by the EMS team, I was feeling off. But I was so excited to see my mom. I cried harder than I had in a really long time.

"I was so scared, Mom, but then I just asked God to take me into Heaven if I didn't make it out of there. Look at that building!"

She turned and looked at the bricks and roof on fire. Before we could say too much, there was an explosion that sent shock waves under my feet. And she held me even closer.

"I love you, Hailey. I know I may compare you to Hayden a lot, and I guess I have to realize you're your own person. I want you to know I'm proud of you, and I'm glad you're alive." She gave me a heartfelt kiss that melted on my head like sweet butter seeps into warm bread.

"I know, Mom. I'm happy to be breathing, too. That guy saved my life," I said, rubbing my own heart, as I loved feeling it beating.

"Which guy, sweetie?" she asked.

"He's over there. He's running for SGA President against Teddi. So it's a lot." Her eyebrows raised, feeling the tough place I was in. "Our floor was locked, and we didn't know how we were gonna get out of there. He stopped and risked his life for us. Then Teddi was unconscious. I—"

Grabbing my hand, she said, "Okay, okay, calm down."

Other people from our building came over to make sure I was fine. With both Teddi and Covin out of that building, I was much better. My mom had me talk to my dad on the phone. He was out of town on military business.

About ten minutes later, I said, "Mom, the guy who risked his life for ours is awesome."

Squinting her eyes at me to make sure I was all right, she said, "Yes, he's a hero for sure."

"I gotta go talk to him. He was pretty out of it when we first came out of the building."

"Well, yeah, you go talk to him if he's able. I'll go find your uncle, and I want to make sure Teddi is okay. Hailey, please stand back, and don't get too close."

As I walked closer to Covin, he stood up as he saw me coming. "No, no, just relax," I told him.

"It's okay. I'm a little weak, but I'm cool," he said when I saw his leg bandaged up. "Plus, my leg is stiffening. Before I go to the hospital I needed to stand. Also, I have to stand for a lady."

I just trembled. It was the oddest day for feelings I hadn't felt in a while. I had never been more drawn to a guy before. As I stood before Covin, knowing he had risked his life for mine, the feelings I had for him were overwhelming. Yeah, I'd had boyfriends before and had had deep feelings for them, but these emotions were different. It was weird. My heart couldn't stop beating fast, and it felt scary to feel connected to someone I barely knew.

He reached out for my hand, and when we clasped he looked deep into my eyes and said, "I'm glad we came out of that building alive."

"I don't know if you heard me, but I'm glad you risked your life for mine and my best friend."

He joked, "Well, when I run against Teddi in the elections next week, I didn't want her to be too mad at me."

"Well, after today you just might have my vote," I smiled and said without really thinking.

He smiled, and his teeth were perfect. Not only were they white, but they were superstraight. They were so inviting, just like his juicy lips. They weren't wet or dry, just naturally moist. I was losing it until he looked at me as if I'd said something wrong.

"I was just joking. You know I'm gonna vote for my girl," I said quickly as I snapped out of it.

"Well, we got a week, and I'm going to do everything I can to change your mind," he said, squeezing my hand a little tighter.

I looked over in Teddi's direction, and she gave me the meanest look. Glad to see she was okay, however, I quickly realized how this looked. She had been unconscious, and to her it seemed like I was consorting with the enemy. But thanks to the enemy, she was breathing.

I quickly let go of Covin's hand and said, "Thank you so much."

"No thanks necessary. I did what I felt I had to do. After the hospital I know I'm going to crash."

I didn't want to leave his side. I did feel like I owed him, but there was something else connecting the two of us. Though I'd let go of his hand, it seemed like we were still touching. That was a hard feeling to shake, and I wasn't sure I wanted to let it go. I was alive, and I was glad to care about life. Covin Randall had my thanks, and maybe something else, too. Nah! I was just overly grateful. No way I could really be into him, right?

\* \* \*

Thirty minutes had passed, and we were all still out there. Tears flowing from everywhere. Many in disbelief of the ordeal others had gone through. Attendance was being taken for those who had residency in the dorm building. Ninety of us had lived on three floors. Thankfully, only a third of us were there at the time the blaze lit. And everyone was accounted for. Finally, the terrible crisis was over.

Then the head custodian of the entire school frantically drove his golf cart over to my uncle. "President Webb! President Webb! My custodian employee, Mayzee King—I haven't been able to find her. I called her house, and she wasn't there. She was working in this building."

Western Smith had approximately fifteen hundred students, and it seemed like double that amount of people were out there. My mother and I were close enough to my uncle to hear what was going on. My heart sank just like a cruise line ripped apart in the ocean. There had to be a rational explanation to where Ms. King was. She had to be alive somewhere in the crowd. The thought of someone perishing in this fire was unbearable.

Covin and a few of his friends came rushing over. Covin said, "We saw our building's custodian. She was the one who told us to get out."

"Yeah," said Jake, who was standing behind Covin. "The lady came in my room and said somebody left a hot plate on, and the fabric on the window treatment was on fire. She said we needed to get everybody out of the building. The fire was spreading."

Campus security came over at the same time to ask

some questions. Officer Hartford said, "So when you guys went to the stairs, you didn't see which way Ms. King went?"

"No," they said together.

Cassidy came over to my uncle. I hadn't seen Cassidy, the Beta, since she'd told me Covin was out of the building. Seeing all the camaraderie of her sorority sisters behind her, I could see they had something special. Why she was living in the dorm and not in the apartment with the Chapter President, who was supposedly her best friend, I didn't know. But I did like seeing about eight Betas who were happy Cassidy was okay.

Cassidy said, "Yeah, the housekeeper was on the second floor. She came to my door and told me to knock on people's doors to get everybody out."

My uncle asked, "And did you see her get out with you guys?"

"No, we were trapped. I assumed she was already on the other side of the door."

"And that's when we came and we heard screams coming from the second floor," Covin said. "There was a beam that had already fallen, and my friends and I were able to move it together. We didn't get out of the building immediately because we made sure everyone on the third floor was out. The second floor got so cloudy so quick—that's why Teddi passed out. Maybe Ms. King got trapped there."

"Oh, my gosh!" I screamed out.

My uncle went and spoke to the fire chief. Flames were lowering, and the firefighters were coming out of the building—or what was left of it anyway. It seemed like they were deliberating for hours, but, actually, only fifteen minutes passed. As the smoke filled the air, it was like God knew what we needed, because it started to rain. Boy, was that a good thing to clear up this smoke. Nobody was going anywhere. Everyone wanted to know what had happened to the lady who'd saved us all.

Finally, my uncle shook his head and looked to the crowd. "If I could just have everyone's attention for a second. Even though it's raining, we are still deeming this an unsafe area. I just want to share this news and then ask you all to vacate the premises. There were a lot of heroes today and brave students who helped each other get out of the building—the firefighters who came quickly and put out the fire, the campus security for keeping everyone in order and for notifying parents. But more than anybody, Ms. Mayzee King, who did die tragically in this fire, risking her life to make sure young people were safe. Western Smith is forever in debt to this brave woman."

I just looked above as the smoke rose and rain fell on my face. Deep in my heart I asked God to take care of the woman who had taken care of all of us. Why her and not me, I would never know. But if I could do anything to help anyone the rest of my life, I would live my life like Mayzee King and help other people to show her I was truly thankful.

The next couple days were extremely tough—tougher, actually, than a steak that has been overcooked. My mom wanted me to come home, but I felt I needed to stay on campus and be with the students. As we held candlelight vigils for Ms. King, we found out a lot about her. She was thirty and had three kids, all under the age of six. She had lived in the most impoverished part of our small town, and her kids didn't have much, and now they'd lost everything because their mom was gone.

I remembered daily feeling ill just thinking about Teddi being a senior in high school, graduating without her parents seeing her. They had been taken in the blink of an eye; her world had just changed forever. She had been practically grown and set in her ways. Yet she needed a little refining, and our friendship helped us both grow. But she wasn't a baby. Ms. King's kids had already lost one parent. We'd found out these kids' dad was in jail for armed robbery and murder, for shooting the clerk of the store he was robbing. No father, and now they didn't have a mother.

Cassidy, Teddi, and I put a sign about the vigil on our new dorm door—where our rooms were across from each other. "There's another vigil tonight. Are you gonna go?" Cassidy asked me.

Teddi had been so shaken up since the incident, I didn't know if she was coming or going. She couldn't sleep at night, and I was becoming extremely concerned. "I'm going to wait for Teddi," I said to Cassidy, knowing she should be back from class by now.

"Well, it's right in front of our building. Y'all need to get out. I see how well you take care of Teddi. I remember you went back to get something from her room the day of the fire. You put yourself in harm's way to help her out. No matter how strong you are, Hailey Grant, I know this is affecting you. We were in that fiery building. We felt the heat of the flames. We saw the red-orange, thick flicker charging at us like it wanted to win. We couldn't breathe inside. I know you thought about what it would be like to perish." I dropped my head, and the tears I had been fighting back came out like a cabinet that was too full to close. "We're scarred for life, Hailey. We won't ever be able to get it out of our mind, but we've got to do something about it. Collectively coming together and going to God, we will get through it."

Wiping my face, I nodded. I went over to the desk and left Teddi a note letting her know I was here.

"I can introduce you to my boyfriend. He's right over there," Cassidy said, pointing to her beau.

"Oh, really? Your boyfriend goes to Western Smith?" I teased as I shoved her a little in the arm.

"Nope. He's a local minister at the youth church not far from here. You should go with me sometime."

"I just may have to do that."

We went to her handsome guy, and she introduced us. He told me to stay strong and that he'd be praying for me. I truly needed to hear that. After I met Rev. Black, he took the stage and started inspiring the sad crowd. His words actually helped.

"You know, it's like we like to have things given to us. 'What can you do for me?' We often ask. Or 'You scratch my back, and I'll scratch yours' is what they said back in the day. Or what about 'What have you done for me lately?' This is another standard we hold people by. But Mayzee King was a lady who, though she had a lot to live for, knew she had a bigger calling to care about others more than she cared about herself. Talking to her mom, I now know she knew God, so I'm not sad that she's done with the troubles of this world. She's in a much better place than we can dream of, but she left us a standard set so high. And I hope everyone whose flame is flicking tonight understands that you gotta give more than you take, and you gotta set up treasures in heaven because you never know when the day's gonna be your last."

The powerful young minister prayed for us, and then Covin took the stage. It had been the first time I'd seen him since the accident. He was strong but clearly shaken.

Covin said, "I'm just gonna be frank with you guys, but I'm sure y'all heard that the King family doesn't have the money to bury Ms. Mayzee. I don't know if y'all have to call home, dig into your own savings, give up your job earnings, sell some stuff, or whatever, but she gave her life for some of us. . . . We will help."

Covin went on to say a few other things, and I was impressed. I certainly had four hundred eighty-five dollars in the bank, and all of it would go to her cause. Covin was definitely the kind of leader our school needed. But no one was moving. Covin had put out a challenge, and we needed to step up.

I went up to the stage and wrote out a check. Covin looked stunned, but he nodded in appreciation. He waved my check in the air, and, thankfully, people started writing checks on the spot and pulling out cash. We had no collection plate, but Covin pulled the hat from his head and turned it upside down.

Covin continued. "Western Smith, that's what I'm talk-ing about. Mayzee King gave her life for ours. Anything extra we raise will go toward her family. Let's all stay com-mitted to helping them. When folks are in need, you give all you have, and this is how you truly show gratitude."

# PARADIGM

"We are the standard for the future. Western Smith's students are an example and a model for what young people all across the country should be like. Sure, we have fun, don't get me wrong, but we're here to get an education. We're here to take it to the next level. We stand for what's right, and we fall for no bull," Covin said as his election speech followed Teddi's the next week.

As hard as I tried not to be connected to him, and as much as I didn't want to be moved by the feelings he was making me feel, I was unsuccessful. I tried to remain unbiased, but it was impossible. He was an orator who had the crowd and me yelling, screaming, moved, and, most importantly, behind him. Teddi and I were over off to the wing. She had just given a pretty lame speech compared to Covin's. She had been nice to thank the crowd for their support during her crisis, and she'd talked about how she planned to get the student body active and re-vived.

Now Teddi shoved me and then walked off stage. I didn't even get to hear what else Covin had to say, but I knew it was going to be well received. And I hated that I actually had to miss it, because I was being inspired. But she was mad, and I guess rightfully so because I was her best friend, her campaign manager, but, most importantly, her girl—like a sister. Honestly speaking, I didn't think she had a chance, and I wasn't sure if she was getting my vote.

"Teddi, girl! Wait up," I said to her as I pulled her arm before she left the library, where the election rally was being held.

"No, don't waste your time running after me. Why don't you go back in there and listen to Covin's lame lies?" Teddi vented; she was near tears.

"What do you mean, lame lies? You heard what he said. It wasn't like he promised anything he wouldn't be able to deliver. He just made everybody feel like we're impor-tant. And that SGA wouldn't be a dictatorship, it would be something that we all can be involved in. I'm sorry if I was excited by what he said." She just started shaking her head and turned her head away from me. "What? You don't want me to tell you the truth? You want me to sugarcoat everything? Come on, Teddi. That's not fair."

I knew that was really what she wanted, but I had to toughen her up. Cassidy was right—I tried to be Teddi's mom. And that wasn't my job. I was her friend. And friends were supposed to be able to give constructive criticism to one another.

"It's your fault I'm not as strong a candidate," she said, stopping in her tracks to let me have it.

Not backing down, because I was upset also, I said, "What do you mean it's my fault?"

"Because you're my campaign manager. If my speech was weak, you should've helped me get it stronger."

"I told you you needed to add more fire to what you were saying," I defended.

"Do you have to use that word, Hailey?" Teddi's eyes welled as if a faucet were just turned on.

I was really frustrated at that moment. I knew we had gone through a lot. But I didn't want every time I made the association with flames, heat, or fire—for goodness sake—to be damned to hell. Or for Teddi to think I was being insensitive to what we had both gone through. Yes, she and Covin had had to go to the hospital to be completely checked out. But I had also had a follow-up doctor's visit. I was still traumatized. But I had to keep living, and I couldn't walk on eggshells with my every word.

Teddi saw in my eyes I didn't appreciate her demeanor. "Just leave me alone, okay? You don't care about me. Leave me alone."

I wanted to shake her and say, "How dare you say I don't care about you? I risked my life for you and would do it again in a heartbeat." Part of my heart was broken that she couldn't see that. But before I could say anything to her, she was gone.

The day didn't get any better once the results were in. Though I wasn't in front with her, I could see her face from the crowd and tell she was pretty devastated when her name wasn't called as our next student-body president. But the crowd loved the fact that Covin's name was announced, and I was so proud of him. He made everyone believe we were special, believe we were the best around, and believe we could do big things. I knew politicians spouted a lot of bull, but because I had seen him in action on the most adversarial day of his life, he was the standard. I knew he was for real, and he deserved to be president.

Though Teddi ran off the stage, and I would have to deal with our differences, she was gonna be okay. Because at the end of the day, the best candidate had won.

"Hailey, are you heading to class? Do you mind if I walk with you?" Cassidy startled me two days after the yucky election as I came out of my dorm room not really paying attention to what was going on around me.

The reason I was so out of it was because I was bummed that Teddi and I were living together but not speaking. This was the first time our tight bond had serious tension. Though I didn't think she was the better candidate, my heart ached for her pain. Well, that was before she started rolling her eyes and labeling her stuff in the room and did things that really irritated me. I was about to knock some sense into the little chick.

As for Cassidy, I was ready to go to class and not be bothered. I wanted to say, "Walk me to class—are you serious? I am not in the sociable mood?" But what was wrong with me stepping out and extending my friendship?

"Sure, yeah. I don't have that far of a walk, though.

These dorms are way closer to my classes than the last dorm was. One of the few blessings in the ordeal we had," I said.

Cassidy said, "I know, right? Classes usually start on the hour. We got about twenty minutes if your class is really close. I was just wondering if me, you, and my friends could have coffee, tea, muffins, or something over at the café."

I wasn't a muffin or tea kinda girl, but I was intrigued. "Sure, I got a little time. You wanna give me a heads-up?"

"Well, you know I'm a Beta like your sister, Hayden, whom we all admire. I don't know what she told you about our chapter, but we had a pretty large line last year. The line I was on. There were a lot of Betas on campus." I didn't know where she was going with this, but I kept listening. "We just wanna talk to you about sorority stuff, if that's okay."

Then I had a confused look on my face. I didn't think it was legal to talk to me in private about sorority stuff. Whatever they might be thinking, I was not up for it.

"Don't worry. No hazing or anything like that. That's why we wanna talk to you in a public place. Just a normal cup of coffee."

As soon as we got to the café, there were five other Betas waving us over. Cassidy motioned for me to take a seat. "You want something to drink?" she said. "I'll get it."

"No, I'm fine," I told her.

"Hi, I'm Samantha," said this girl I recognized as she looked me over.

"I know you. You're the new Chapter President, right?"

"Yes." She smiled and nodded approvingly because I knew her position.

A few other girls coughed and looked at each other. I didn't know what was going on, but I knew it was something internal.

Samantha turned to them and then looked at me. "Sorry about that," she said. "It's hard to recruit people. We are thinking about having a line, and we want to let you know we think you're dynamic."

"Yeah," Cassidy said. "I told them about everything that happened when we were in the fire. So many girls are jocking us, wanting to be down with Beta Gamma Pi, not having a clue about what it means to put others above yourself."

"And we want girls with character," Samantha said. "Girls who don't mind going against the grain or standing with the minority because they'd rather do what's right, even if it means standing alone. We just plan to put a few on our line this year. We just want to ask you to come to our rush. We plan to do it strictly by the book. Really true sisterhood and get a lot of great bonding going on. So, you know, we hope it works out because we'd really like to have you join BGP." Then they got up and walked out.

I noticed Teddi standing by the door as they left. She came to me and said, "Were the Betas sitting with you?"

I knew she wanted to be a Beta. Most of the girls at our school did, so I believed them when they said young women were practically begging them. But Teddi hadn't even been speaking to me. And now all the interest.

"Have the Betas talked to *you?*" I asked because I knew if they hadn't reached out to Teddi, I didn't want to throw it in her face that I was their top pick and she wasn't.

"What did they want with you?" she asked, again speaking to me for the first time in a couple of days.

I knew she couldn't take any more disappointment, so I said, "You know, just being sorority girls."

"Yeah, I know. Trying to tell you how to act and stuff. Cool it down and not be such a maverick. They don't have to tell me how to act like a Beta. I studied them all last year. I learned their ways. I'm ready."

I just nodded.

False as the hope was, it was certainly good to see her feel confident again. And as salty as I was with her for being mad at me for having my own mind, I knew I loved her deeply, and as much as I appreciated their flattery, I would much rather enjoy seeing Teddi as a Beta than me. Maybe I would lose my interest if that happened.

"So the Betas want you to pledge, huh, lil' sis?" Hayden said to me as we sat down for dinner.

We hadn't had sister time in over a few months, which was so odd because we'd used to get together every week. But she had her off-and-on-boyfriend, Creed, since her days at Western Smith. Whenever I'd called her over the summer to hang out and do this or that, she would shoot me down with how she couldn't or she and Creed had plans, so I just stopped asking. Then out of the blue she'd wanted to take me out to eat, but I knew why. She wanted to talk about the Betas.

"Let me just stop you," I said to her before the waiter came over to our table. "Yeah, the Betas talked a good game, and that was cool and everything, but—"

"But? Are you kidding? For them to say you're who

they're looking for and all you need to do is apply is unheard of. They usually give girls a hard time."

"I don't want any special treatment. I don't want people coming up to me telling me I'm who they're looking for. The only reason they stepped up to me is because I'm your younger sister. Did you call them and tell them they better put me on the line, Hayden?"

"Girl, they hate legacies," she said as she looked around for the waiter. "We've been sitting around for twenty minutes. I'm thirsty. Besides, you're a double legacy. Your mom and your sister are Betas. In my days on campus that was not cool. If they talked to you, something you did stood out."

My sister was very strong. I didn't know a lot about her pledge days, but I remembered it was brutal. Girls were hazed pretty badly. She had been on some underground line that had gotten dropped. A girl had ended up in the hospital, and an alumni chapter had had to take over. Because some girls had gotten suspended, the new girls were the only ones on campus. They'd elected Hayden for Chapter President, and that had worked great for a minute, but her strong-willed personality had ended up alienating them.

The waiter came over and took our order. As bad as my sister had wanted the waiter over, now she was kinda rushing him off so we could talk more. Before Hayden could open her mouth I said, "Don't sell me on Beta Gamma Pi. I wanna see for myself. I wanna try out some other organizations. I'm not sure if pledging is for me at all anyway."

She grabbed my hand and said, "Yes. I know you re-member that my pledging experience was difficult, but a lot has changed. Again, they're not trying to take you to some dark room and jack you up. They intimidated the heck out of me. I only pledged because I knew it was in my heart. I wanted to be like Mom so badly and have a good underground experience, but that's not what I had."

"You wanted to have an underground experience?" I asked her.

"I meant undergrad experience because, you know, Mom pledged grad chapter. Truthfully, if I had to do it over again, I wish I would've pledged as a grad because pledging was a lot of work, but right now the Betas have their heads on straight, and they plan to do it right for your line. They want only a few girls, and they want you, Hailey. They know a good thing when they see one. You are so awesome, Hailey. I am just excited. Tickled purple and turquoise—Beta Gamma Pi colors, okay—that they want my little sister to be a part of our sisterhood. You're so strong and care about yourself; you could be a great leader."

"Yeah, right. You tried for a position within the na-tional office, and I saw what it did to you."

Hayden thanked the waiter as she sipped her water with lemon. Then she said, "Yeah, but I didn't win. The President appointed me to a national committee, and it's been great serving. You could go all the way because you have vision. People like you. If you need to try out other organizations by going to their rushes or talking to them, I support that. I don't wanna cram what I know to be the best down your throat. I feel confident to say that if you go and check out the others, you're gonna want to come to Beta Gamma Pi. Because when it's done right, we are the stuff. We are the standard. We are the paradigm."

# BIASED

"I know what sorority I wanna be in," Teddi said to me as I got ready to go to Rho Tau Nu's rush.

"That's great, girl. I haven't decided if pledging is for me, but I owe it to myself to go and give everybody a chance and figure out if it's even something I want."

"What, Hailey? Girl, you are a legacy, and I'm not one. There's nobody in my family who is a Beta, but I know BGP is it for me. You should know that better than anybody," Teddi said, almost salty that my mind wasn't made up.

"Well, I don't, okay? I know what it's like firsthand from my mom and my sister. It's not all smiles. I've seen their tears. I just wanna see if there is another sorority I can gel with."

"You're just gonna be committing suicide if you do that, girl. The Betas aren't gonna want you if they see you trying out everything in the world."

"If that's the case, it wasn't right for me to pledge Beta Gamma Pi. Besides, it was my sister who encouraged me to get out there and see for myself. She felt confident that I was gonna pick her sorority. If she isn't sweating it, why should you?"

Teddi came over to me and grabbed both of my hands. "Look, I know we've been distant for the past weeks, and I've been really angry with you. The last thing I want is for us to keep having distance like we have. We're sisters. Not sorority sisters, not blood sisters, but we are sisters connected at the heart, and I want us to experience some things together. We talked about coming to college together to do this stuff. We don't take classes together. We don't do any extracurriculars together. Can't we try to get our bond back? Am I the only one who wants that?"

Needing to have a really tough conversation with her, I frankly said, "Wait. Stop, Teddi. We don't take any classes together because I'm in pre-law, and you're in education. Our scholastic paths don't even cross like that."

"Well, we were gonna do stuff with SGA. You were supposed to be in my cabinet. Now there's a message on my door from the new President saying he wants to meet with you tomorrow. What's that about, Hailey?"

"Really?" I questioned in a shocked tone. "I'm not going to be able to meet with him tomorrow."

"Yeah, I'm sure you're gonna reschedule," she said, handing me the Post-it note with great handwriting.

"I may or may not. Teddi, let it go. Come on, you're my girl. I know we wanna do stuff together, and we will. But we're still individuals. We gotta make our own way."

"You know a lot of things, Hailey Grant, but you don't have to go to other rushes to see that the other sororities don't compare to BGP. But don't take it from me. Go."

An hour later, while I was at the Rho Tau Nu rush, all they were talking about was how they wished they were doing this like the Betas and they wished they were doing that like the Betas. I realized they needed to stop wishing and get up and do something. The image of them around campus was that they were made up of a bunch of insecure girls. As I looked around the room, it wasn't ugliness in the room, it was just girls who had a lack of self-worth. I didn't even stay for the whole thing.

The next night when I went over to the Mu Eta Mu rush, I ran into Covin.

He stopped me and said, "So I got your message that you wouldn't be able to meet with me, but you're out here on campus alone. You don't seem busy to me."

"I'm heading somewhere as we speak."

"Okay, how about next week? I really need to talk to you," he insisted.

"Is it gonna take a long time?" I asked.

"I don't wanna rush what it is I have to say, if that's what you're asking."

"Yeah, technically, I guess that is what I'm asking," I said as I looked over his shoulder and saw the Mu sorors were looking around to see if anyone else was coming. "But I'm headed somewhere now, so I gotta jet."

"Give a brother a chance, Miss Lady. Call me sometime," he said as he moved out of my way.

"We're closing the doors! We're closing the doors, and

you will be shut out if you're not in here!" the Mu Eta Mu Vice President shouted out to girls who were trying to come inside.

The Mus didn't even speak to anyone as we interested girls all mingled about. This group of gals was the exact opposite of where I had been the night before. They didn't lack confidence— they were overly confident. Yeah, they had on cute clothes, but all they talked about was how inferior the interested girls were. My thought was if you were all that as a sorority, you don't need to bash anyone else. This definitely wasn't me, and, again, I could not stay.

Two nights later, it was the Beta rush. Teddi and I went, and every girl walking into their dorm room was super-excited. Except me. I wasn't uninterested, but I wasn't completely sold either.

Teddi and I both stopped in our tracks when we saw a very attractive girl arguing with this thug-looking dude. I knew it was none of our business, but he was getting extra-loud with her. She tried to head toward the Betas' door, and he grabbed her sassy hair.

"Evan, I'm letting you do this sorority thing, but it better pay off for me, and it sure better not take too much of your time," he told her as he let her go.

It was dark, and I could not see the girl's face. But she looked around and seemed so embarrassed. Very weird that she should have been checking ole boy instead of making sure no one saw him be overly aggressive.

Teddi said, "No, she ain't kissing that jerk. See, y'all, black women need to stop putting up with crazy behavior just to have a man."

The Evan girl went past us, and I was feeling like I

should let her know she deserved more. But she didn't look at me, so I knew she didn't want my input. Plus, Teddi tugged on my arm because it was time for the Beta rush to begin.

They were organized, they were inviting, and they talked about how they wanted to make the world better. They complimented us, and they mentioned other leaders. True sisters. Smart women. Women who loved the Lord, and women who wanted to make a difference. I loved seeing their room decked out with so much past history of women who have made a difference locally, regionally, nationally, and internationally. All these things were a part of me. The Betas were together, and I was proud of my African American sisters.

I still wasn't sure if pledging was for me. However, my sister was right. I had tried others, and they didn't measure up to Beta Gamma Pi. If I was going to do this sorority thing, clearly, BGP was my only choice.

"Okay, so what did you want to meet with me about?" I said to Covin when we met on a Friday night as we sat at the finest restaurant in town.

"Dang, you won't even cut a brother some slack. Can we enjoy the evening first? I just wanna get to know you for a second before we dive right into business."

"Well, we don't need to waste any time. You said you needed my help, and I'm here. I have a tough course load this semester, and I'm thinking about adding another activity that will take up more of my time. I don't wanna waste yours. Tell me what it is you need so I can see if I can help."

I tried to sound as tough as I could to fight the queasiness I was feeling. His hazel eyes matched his skin, and with every word he said it was like his lips were calling mine. I was not gonna be drawn into sweet talk and a handsome face. Or at least with everything in me I was going to fight off the feeling.

I thought we were gonna talk business, so I was taken aback when he said, "I'm the student-body president of this campus, and I have a tough course load myself. I should be focused on my hopes and dreams, but I'm not. I can't stop thinking about your beautiful face that kept me going through the fire. A lot of people have talked about helping me, wanting this position and that position, and I'm going to see what I can do. A lot of girls have been throwing a lot of stuff at me, too, but I can see through many facades. When I needed someone to come along beside me and help Ms. Mayzee's family, you stood up and took the lead. You made a difference. You touched my heart. I never got to tell you thanks. So many people in this life wanna take charge, like my dad, who I admire. But you stepped out and made a difference."

"That's kind. But your dad does a lot. He's state senator, right? He's making a huge difference for us," I said respectfully.

"Yeah, he really is. He had told me I need to look for people to be in my corner that give more than they take. He also told me it was high time I started looking for a girlfriend. Though he told me my mom would help me in that department, I assured him I'd be all right. I always figured a girlfriend would come whenever she came. I wasn't looking for a girl I would fall for, but, Hailey—

wow, I even love saying your name. It's like heaven to me, you know. You're something special. Up until tonight, I thought you were attracted to me, too, and if you tell me I'm wrong, I won't bother you. We can make our relationship only business because you got something special I need to help make my administration count."

I batted my eyes while looking at the table because I couldn't look at him anymore. My heart was racing like a sports car on the expressway. I needed to cool down. I felt overheated. So I looked away, almost uninterested.

He took the hint and changed the subject. I felt more comfortable listening to him going on and on about becoming President of the United States one day. But then when he said he could see me as his First Lady because I had class, grace, dignity, and soul, I lost it again. When he touched my hands I almost couldn't contain myself, but I bit my nails instead, as I often did when I got nervous.

Sensing me pulling back again, he said, "Seems I'm barking up the wrong tree here. So let's forget the personal conversation and get to the professional stuff. I really wanted to come to you and offer the position of director of community relations. We have cabinet meetings only once a month, so that will go well with what you got going on already. The only other responsibilities you'd have is to plan an event for the fall and spring, and I'd even be okay if we continued to help Ms. Mayzee King's family. Don't feel uneasy. You won't have to worry about me getting romantic with you again."

The waiter came with our food. I liked that Covin asked to lead with a prayer. Though I wasn't the strongest Christian, I knew I was impressed that the guy before me had given respect to the Lord. With my head bowed and my eyes closed, so many thoughts were running through my head. I didn't want him to get the wrong idea about me not appreciating what he had to say. I was truly in tune with his heart, too, and wanted our communication to grow. However, I had never had a guy in my life who was so open and honest with me from the start, and it felt good. Taking this position would cause many conflicts, but I had to look out for my own interests.

Raising my head from the prayer, I said, "I would really love to be the director of community relations. I do have a heart for kids on this campus and helping to make this city better. But I can accept only if you and I can continue to explore what we may have. You didn't read me wrong; I am attracted to you. And maybe that's what is making me act like I didn't have any feelings, because I'm a little . . ." I didn't even wanna say I was nervous.

When I looked down, the next thing I knew he was standing beside me. He lifted my chin, and he bent down and gave me a gentle kiss on my cheek. I felt tingles all over my body. I couldn't believe I was his pick.

Autumn was flying by, and ten days had passed. Covin and I were having a great time dating. We'd meet in the library to study and get down to business. I was helping him not only with my responsibilities as community-relations director but giving him my thoughts on other parts of his administration as well. His boy, Jake, who was his adviser, was pretty ticked that I had the ear of the President. But Covin and I didn't care. We were connecting, and it felt good.

I was actually able to balance my time more than I thought I would be able to. School, SGA, and love blended well. I had no spare time, but I liked my life. I was full.

Though I was happy with my life, I was getting pressure from my mom, sister, and best friend, who kept asking me to pledge. The pledge packet was due for BGP.

Reluctantly, Teddi convinced me to just turn in my Beta Gamma Pi application, letters of recommendation, and transcript. Though I had no clue whether I was really gonna make line or not, I did at least get them all off my back by trying.

Next thing I knew, I was sitting in an interview in front of eight Western Smith Betas and their adviser. They drilled me with tons of questions. And because the questions were all service related, I soared with my answers. I knew from their smiles that I was winning them over.

When I went back to my own busy life, I got the call from Cassidy. "You've been accepted as a pledge member of Beta Gamma Pi. Meet us at the Historic Theater on campus, upstairs room 202, and bring the necessary funds requested."

Immediately after, I called my mom and told her the news. She was elated. Within hours she was dropping off the cashier's check in the amount of nine hundred and fifty dollars. A big part of me wanted to tell her to save her money, but she kept going on and on about how excited she was that her baby was going to be her sister.

So I kept my appointment to meet the Betas. When I got there, Cassidy and Samantha were seated before me. I wanted to ask Teddi if she had gotten a call from the Betas, but she wasn't picking up her cell, and she wasn't home when I left to go to the bank to pick up the cashier's check.

Just as I was about to hand in my money, Samantha got a call and motioned for Cassidy to come over. Some girl didn't make line and was asking a whole bunch of questions. I didn't mean to pry, but I could see the clipboard that held only four names. The line had three other girls I didn't know, but I didn't see Teddi's name there. I became really upset. I just knew she wasn't going to be chosen. She wanted this more than me.

As soon as Samantha hung up the phone, they came back over to me. I couldn't play it off. "Listen, guys, I appreciate you all wanting me. Um, and as you say, Betas are leaders. Though I'm not a Beta now, I took it upon myself to view the table, and I noticed the list of girls you want to bring into the fold. Teddi Spencer, my roommate, isn't on there."

"Yeah, her name's not on there because we can't choose a lot of people," Cassidy said, knowing how deeply I cared about my girl.

Samantha rolled her eyes and had a little tougher response. "Look, we owe no pledge explanations."

"No disrespect, Sam, but you need to know I know she's a way better fit for you all than I am. So I just want to tell you that if spaces are limited, you want to choose her more than me."

"Your loyalty is admirable, Hailey, but, no, we want you," Cassidy said.

"No, I'm telling you you want Teddi. She really wants to serve. She is willing to give you her whole heart. I'm the one who is divided into so many directions, and if you want to choose someone based on space, it's her you want and not me. Please reconsider! I don't know how else to say that Teddi is the girl you need, and if she's not gonna be in it, I don't wanna be in it. I'm sorry."

"That's a pretty bold stand you're taking," Samantha said as I walked toward the door.

"Sometimes people don't know what they need, and it will take a little pushing. If you want me that bad, you're going to have to consider Teddi."

Samantha came to the door and opened it for me. "Well, we're telling you right now that you might be giving up your chance of being a Beta."

As I walked out I said, "That's a risk I'm willing to take. If you don't choose Teddi, you lose me. She is the better choice, and it's a fact. I'm not biased."

# GALORE

I couldn't believe I was standing in a room with three other girls I didn't know to take the first steps toward becoming a member of Beta Gamma Pi. I had been serious when I stood before Cassidy and Samantha and told them to choose Teddi over me, and I had meant it when I said if Teddi didn't do it, I didn't want to be in it. However, someway, somehow I allowed my mother and my sister to convince me not to back out.

I could still hear Hayden now when I told her I wasn't gonna do it if my best friend didn't get an invitation. She'd said, "Girl, please. Sometimes you get in and then bring other people in. Don't trip. You can take your opportunity now, and you can make Teddi a Beta next year." Logically and reasonably enough, I understood.

I still wasn't sure until my mom said, "There are a lot

of things a mother wants for her child. Being a member of my sorority is one of the things I want for you, Hailey. Four years ago I was scared and didn't want Hayden pledging because I knew they weren't planning to do it the right way. But now that things have changed, they wanna go and do it by the book, and they have chosen you to be one they induct into the sorority. Take advantage of it. Look at it as respect and not disloyalty to your girlfriend."

So here I stood wearing white in October, feeling like I was betraying Teddi all over again. I was gonna go through with it, but I felt uneasy about it. I wasn't trying to be standoffish, but I wasn't frolicking with the other three girls either, waiting for whatever the Betas were going to bring us through.

There was a girl who was cute and trendy and looked familiar who came over to me and said, "Hi, my name is Evan Harrison."

A girl with glasses, who didn't seem as fashionable yet had to-die-for Indian-type hair, said, "Hi, I'm Quisa Bland."

Then a spunky, heavyset girl with dreads said, "I'm Millie Foster."

"Evan, Quisa, and Millie," I repeated in the most unexcited voice I could muster. "Nice to meet you all. I'm Hailey Grant."

Quisa looked at her watch and said, "I guess we're gonna start as soon as the other girl gets here."

"Well, she needs to hurry up," Millie said. "I'm ready to get this show on the road. Shoot, I'm hungry."

"And my high-maintenance man—I gotta get to him,"

Evan said as she looked at her watch, which made me realize I remembered her from the Beta rush with her forceful boyfriend.

As the three of them talked about their excitement, I listened on. *Another girl?* I thought. I was so confused until I heard Teddi scream.

"Hailey, you're here! I knew you'd be here. You just had to be! I thought I was never gonna make it. I got lost, and they called me at the last minute and—we're in." She came over and gave me a big hug.

Surely the chapter higher-ups, Sam and Cassidy, hadn't rethought putting her on line for me. They knew from my sister that I was still gonna pledge. How did this happen? But I didn't wanna question. Everything was all cool, now that my girl was here. Being real, I knew deep down Teddi was here because I had made a good case for why they needed her.

"Hey, you guys, isn't this exciting?" Teddi said, bringing the room alive. "I wanted to be a Beta for so long. When I got the call this morning, I was ready! I got my money from my grandmother. I had to go to the store and find the right dress. How do I look? Is this cute?" Teddi showed us all she wanted to make a great impression on the soon-to-be big sisters.

It was obvious Teddi was very excited, but I was nervous. It dawned on me that I had a huge responsibility. The Betas probably valued me so much that they took what I'd said about my friend into consideration and heeded my request. Though being a Beta wasn't my first choice, I certainly was gonna have to make it a priority. I had big respect for them now. Rationalizing all this, it seemed the Betas were so into me they had granted my request. Maybe Hayden hadn't let them know I was coming. Obviously, they had dubbed my worth, and I wasn't gonna let them down.

I introduced Teddi to Evan, Quisa, and Millie and said to the four of them, "I guess we're entering into a unique sisterhood. We gotta get to know each other better. We gotta have our own bond."

We hugged each other and lined up by height when Cassidy came into the room to get us. None of us knew what to expect. But as we walked down a path lit by burning candles and then sat on a pillow one by one and took the oath to become a Pi, we heard and reflected on the song the Betas sang around us. They vowed to treat us with respect and love and to make their world ours so that collectively we could make the community and our great college a better place.

I was overcome with emotion. Holding hands with Teddi, I knew we were in for something big. After the ceremony was over, my mother and sister—with tear-filled eyes—came and told me I'd made a decision to serve that would bless me and many in my lifetime. Feeling the love, I was happy I'd made a choice to be a part of this amazing sorority.

"Okay, so we gotta go to the store and get our clothes so we can dress alike," Teddi said to me as she went on and on about how pumped she was that we were now Pis.

I didn't know the other three girls well, but I could see they were as overwhelmed as I was with Teddi's enthusiasm. She was pumped up enough for all of us. But, again, after the moving ceremony I'd just experienced, I knew I had to dig deep and get fired up about this pledge process, too.

"All right, I'm not saying we gotta dress alike and all that, but break it down to me about this pledge stuff. Particularly because this isn't the old-school way, and we're doing it by the book. We're not supposed to walk in a line and be dressed alike," I said to my friend.

Millie said, "We don't have to be hazed to have a little fun of our own, and as long as we're not going crazy with it, we can dress how we want. Alike does sound fun."

"See, it will be fun. Plus, I think we're giving reverence to the process by being identifiable. Folks will say, 'Look at the five elite girls the Betas chose this year,'" Teddi said, making a good point. "We should represent."

"Well, I don't wanna look like a hag," Evan said. "And I don't have much time to shop. I gotta get to my boo. Besides, what's open?"

I knew if Evan mentioned her crazy guy one more time and the short leash he obviously had her on, I was going to scream. Truly, she was showing anxiety about pleasing this dude. Surely, she was overstressing. What could he do if she was a little late?

"Well, I don't wanna spend a lot of money," Quisa combatted.

Teddi and Millie talked to her, and Evan made a phone call. Finally, after a little more debating, we agreed to get some simple solids. The best place for that was the local discount retailer. It wasn't my shopping place, but for this purpose, I knew it was going to have prices we were all cool with.

"I do not like going to a twenty-four-hour shopping store and not seeing any cars in the parking lot. We need protection," Evan said, letting us all know she didn't get out much without her guy.

Out of all of us, Teddi was the politician. She went over to her and said, "I don't like it either, but this is our first bonding time. We are going to go in and get right out, and tomorrow we're gonna be dressed alike! We won't spend a lot of money or keep anyone long."

"Well, I shop at night. And this place is safe," Millie said as the five of us walked through the dark lot, with most of us looking over our shoulders.

As soon as we got to the store door, bright lights were flashing and nearly blinding us from an out-of-control car. The five of us jumped onto the curb. Evan's face held a petrified glare.

Evan shouted—clearly, she was scared—"That's him, you guys. Please, please, please go on in."

"Do I need to talk to him?" I asked, trying to calm her down. "You seem scared of this dude, Evan, and the way he rolled up on us—no wonder."

"No, I don't need any of y'all to talk to him. Just go in," Evan pleaded.

"I'm not leaving you in the middle of the street," Teddi said.

Evan quickly went up to his car and said, "I'm sorry,

baby. We just had to pick up something for this sorority thing."

Her guy started talking loud, clearly wanting us to hear. "I told you not to be a part of this mess! I'm out there waiting on you, and then I see you getting in the car with your friends! You can't call me after the fact? I followed you here, and now it's time to go. We were supposed to chill tonight!"

"Do you have to yell?" Teddi said, making it her business to head up to his car.

I was all about business, ready to find whatever it was we agreed to and get to bed. It had been a long day, from going through the ceremony to talking later with my mom, sister, and all their alumni friends. Bonding was the most important thing. Of my new sisters, there was the sassy one, the overly outgoing one, the quiet one, a country one, and myself—we were interestingly different, and it was gonna take a lot more nights to know each other better. Tonight was not the night for me though. I was on a mission.

I actually walked across the street beside Teddi. This guy was frightening, and I didn't wanna leave my sisters alone with him for another second. I wasn't sure what made him so scary. Maybe it was his gold teeth or his heavy chains or maybe his chiseled but thuglike stature. I had a gut feeling that he was local and was trying to be harder than he appeared.

"Evan, you better get your friends. I'm not talking to them!" her boyfriend slurred out either high, drunk, or both.

Evan came over to us and said, "Okay, I just need to talk to him and calm him down. Can y'all please go in and get what we need? Please!"

"You don't need to leave with that guy. He's obviously been drinking and very upset," I said, basically beseeching her to come in with us.

"G-Dogg? No, he's cool. He's a little overprotective. Let me square things away, and I'll be right in," Evan said, telling us what we wanted to hear.

Quisa said, "Come on, Hailey. Give her some time with her man. She said she'll be in."

Against my better judgment, the four of us left her outside with that hostile nut. She was hugging him. He looked like a broken-down, old-fashioned, good-for-nothing gangster.

As soon as we stepped inside, Teddi said, "I don't see how we get caught up with these guys, thinking they're our only way out. He ain't got nothing going on for himself. Why is Evan with him?"

"Let's just hurry and get what we need," I told her, really wanting to make certain Evan was cool.

A part of me wanted to stand guard and keep a close eye on Evan. As long as I could I watched her from the door, but when I turned my head for a second and then looked back, she was gone.

His car was there, but they were nowhere in sight. What was up with that? Quickly, I went to get everyone else. Teddi, Millie, and Quisa felt my nervousness. We were only in the store for seven minutes—a record for four young women, I'm sure. We bought white sweat suits, jeans that were alike, and some black shirts.

Stepping back outside, the four of us were devastatingly stunned as G-Dogg brought a left hook down on the right side of Evan's horrified face.

I started second-guessing myself. When I couldn't see them before, were they hidden behind his car so he could rough her up? Had I dashed away when I should have fled to her side? Was it my fault everything was not right with my new friend?

"Oh, no, he didn't!" Teddi said as she took off and tried to fight the guy herself.

"Someone call the cops!" I shouted. "Justice needs to be served on this fool."

Millie said, with tears, "Got you. I'm calling nine-one-one now. You're right, Hailey, he can't beat her up like this!"

"No, no, you guys, the cops are criminals. Don't call them. Please, I can handle him," Evan pleaded as Millie dialed her phone anyway.

*Why did we leave her alone?* I wondered. I felt so bad. Not caring if it was wrong or dangerous to try to jump into the domestic disturbance, I joined my roommate in her quest to get Evan away from the jerk. It took Teddi and me giving all our effort to get him off her.

Evan was speaking, but she wasn't agreeing with us helping her. She was screaming at us for interfering in her business! If we hadn't helped her, she would've ended up in the hospital. Quisa grabbed the security guards from inside the store, and they held G-Dogg down. He went ballistic, telling Teddi and me that we were gonna be sorry. I wanted to yell out, "Kick him, punch him, beat him!"

but I knew that was wrong. The only thing I could do was console my girl.

Evan was calling out for the one who had battered and bruised her. G-Dogg was screaming for the security guards to release him. Inwardly, I was yelling for justice to be done.

So I said to Evan, "Look, you can't think this G-Dogg is good for you, girl! You need to be concerned with yourself. A man should never hit a woman. Take a stand. Don't allow him to ruin your life. Here come the cops. You gotta press charges, or we will."

When the guards handed him over to the cops, G-Dogg reached for something in his pocket. I couldn't make out what it was. But I knew it wasn't a toy.

"You need to surrender your weapon," one of the cops said to G-Dogg.

I don't know if G-Dogg was just that crazy or just that high, but he shot his gun in the air. I grabbed Evan and tugged her out of the way. At that moment, chaos broke out. Teddi, Quisa, and Millie came to my side and hugged me. The events we witnessed next made our horrible night turn even worse.

All four white police started closing in on G-Dogg. Two came up behind him and forced him to the ground. They just started clobbering the boy with their sticks. With a bloody face and busted mouth, I personally, was satisfied. He was contained, but they started beating him some more. People came out of the store and joined us in yelling for them to stop. The cruel po-po wouldn't.

We'd called the cops on this dude so he wouldn't kill our friend, and now it seemed he was being abused. We couldn't win for losing. If Evan wasn't into this G-Dogg character enough, now she was over the top for him. What was I gonna do about all this violence galore?

## PESKY

"That's a violation of his rights hitting him like that!" I yelled out as I charged toward the cops hitting a guy I hated defending—yet I hated him getting beaten even more.

How could I have been so wrong? How could I have trusted the system to take him in and prosecute him the right way? I wanted to be a trial lawyer so I could make a difference. Was I being naive that I trusted the system would uphold justice? Evan tried to tell me that cops in this town didn't treat fairly black men who don't look a certain way. As I looked back at her helpless face, I felt horrible.

"Somebody help him! Somebody call someone!" I screamed out as Teddi and Millie held me back from getting in the middle of the hideous action.

"Why are you trying to help this criminal out?" a bystander yelled out to me. "He hit your friend!"

I'm not saying just because the assailant was black, young, and male that everyone was against him. But I thought it was very ironic that the person telling me to ignore what I was seeing was a white man who seemed happy to throw away the key on another brother.

"Do you think what they're doing to him is right?" I asked the man standing to my left.

"Do you think him discharging a gun is right!" he screamed back at me. "He could have killed someone."

"Don't worry about it. Don't worry about it, Hailey," Millie said with her cell pointed at everyone. "I'm recording all this on my phone. Cops, you all need to stop."

"Get him in the back of the car now and let's take him to the station," one of the cops said to the other. "These are just a bunch of young kids making noise, and they can't do anything."

Teddi said, "With videotape we will do something."

G-Dogg looked worse than Rodney King, who'd suffered police brutality in the early nineties from the Los Angeles police department. G-Dogg had swollen eyes and a distorted, bloody face. You could see in G-Dogg's pitiful, raged eyes, as they stared at the crooked cops, that he'd had his share of dealing with the tough local police department.

Evan cried out, "I hope you guys are happy! G needs to be taken to a hospital, not a precinct. We gotta go help him."

She got no argument from any of us on that. My line sisters and I got back into the car and followed the two police cars with blue lights flashing on both. I was driving a little too fast trailing the police car, but I was upset.

Teddi said, "Slow down, Hailey. I know you're hot. I'm mad, too. The cops were clearly out of line back there. However, you can't get a ticket. Stop following their cars like this. We don't wanna go to jail, too, do we?"

"Look, if we don't stand for something, we'll fall for anything," I told her. "I'm the one who said to call the police. I'm the one who wanted justice and expected it would be done. Then those cops, who are racist and nasty for whatever reasons, who took us backward and not forward, are going to be held accountable for their actions. Calling us some kids who can't do anything—we'll show them. Shoot, I can't even find my cell phone."

"It's right here in your purse," Teddi said as she handed it to me. "What are you doing?"

I said, "We need to call everybody we know and tell them to meet us here at the station. And somebody needs to call the TV crew."

It was two in the morning, and I felt bad waking Covin up. No, I didn't feel bad at all. I knew he had to get up. I needed his help, and when he heard what I had to say, he showed himself once again to be the man I admired. He met us at the police station with about forty students strong.

We started chanting, "The police are wrong! The police are wrong!"

Our outraged group kept getting louder and louder. When the television crew showed up we were even more boisterous and demanded a difference. We were interviewed and showed them the videotape of the beating. The news crew and reporters went inside and got answers. We waited and would not go away.

When the news crew came back out, it was evident they were with us and believed we weren't blowing smoke. There was a large fire ablaze in the police department. The anchor woman I recognized from TV admitted someone was trying to cover up what had really happened. Evan and I pleaded with her that we could not let that happen.

The TV woman, Lysa Ford, said, "I'm sure we'll see some action in our favor. This department cannot take another racial incident."

Covin went into the station. He assured Evan everything was going to be all right. Whatever his idea was, I was moved that he cared enough to try to help.

About thirty minutes later, Covin came out of the building smiling. The police chief and the four officers who were involved followed. Ms. Ford rushed up to the chief with her microphone. The chief announced that the four officers were going to be suspended without pay, pending an investigation. The officers passed us and looked severely disturbed.

The ring leader who had called us kids looked at us and said, "We know that guy. You all want us suspended, but we're only protecting the neighborhood."

Close enough to read his name badge, I said, "Officer Cloud, now you see we are not just some kids with no voice. I'm the first to admit that guy is no saint. But the way you treated him was not right. You are supposed to uphold the law. Now, like you wanted the guy to pay, you'll have to pay."

He looked away. I hadn't meant to sound so cruel.

Passing back to him the anger he'd made me feel wasn't healthy.

An ambulance arrived, and G-Dogg came out of the precinct in handcuffs and was escorted to it. Evan fled to his side. Like a gnat that wouldn't go away, this nagging feeling told me to tell him I was sorry. Teddi and Millie saw I was headed to them. They tried to keep me back from the action, but while the news crew entertained my line sisters, I went over to see the guy who had threatened my girl's life.

"I apologize," I told him as I looked at his face that was so unrecognizable from the earlier jerk. "You deserve to be locked up—"

Evan said, "Hailey—"

My voice rattled, I said, "What, Evan? He was wrong to hit you."

"Ladies, he's under arrest," a dark-skinned officer said to Evan and me. "He's not able to talk to anyone at this time."

G-Dogg looked at the cop with empathy. "Hey, bro, can I have a minute?"

The officer hesitated and then nodded. He uncuffed G-Dogg and stepped to the side. Evan put her free arms around his waist.

Surprising me, G-Dogg pulled back and said, "Your girl is right, baby. I never should have touched you. Hitting you was wrong."

Like someone who needed sense knocked into them—no pun intended—Evan said, "I deserved it. I made you angry. Now, because of me, look at you. You're gonna need stitches."

"Evan!" I yelled out, wishing she wasn't so gullible.

The paramedic I remembered from the fire, told us he needed to get the patient to the hospital. I backed away, and Evan held on to his neck for dear life. The officer came between Evan and G-Dogg.

I motioned for Evan to come with me. She was obviously mad at me and ran over to Millie and Quisa. I looked to the sky and needed God to help me not feel so bad, even though I felt I was just trying to help.

When the cop and paramedic were closing the door, G-Dogg said, "Please take care of my girl." I turned and looked back at him. "I was wrong to hit her, but when the cops went too far, you stood up for me. Thank you. I'm ready to take on the judge, lawyers, and whoever else wants to throw the book at me. Tonight I learned about compassion when I looked over at your face and saw how much you were hurting for me—me, the guy who got rough with your friend. I was numb to the brutality and hate they were giving me. I owe you. You showed me goodness. I gotta change. And I'm glad Evan is in a group or sorority with you."

When the ambulance pulled off, I sat there. I felt strong arms touching me. The rub was so soothing I knew it was Covin. He was around me taking care of things, setting the record straight. Right now I felt safe because I was in his reach. I slowly turned around, and our eyes locked. I couldn't keep it together anymore. I completely fell apart in his arms. He held me up, he told me it was gonna be okay, and he didn't leave.

Covin had told me that pledging could be brutal, but he didn't know the Betas had planned on doing it the right way. I was out in the wee hours of the morning only because my line sisters and I wanted to hang. Covin could have given me much scolding, but he told me what I wanted to hear.

"I'm so glad you're okay. I'm glad you called me," he said as he rubbed my brow with a touch that felt so secure.

He kissed my forehead and then my cheek. When his juicy lips met mine, I did feel better. I had just gone through a nightmare. And I needed that awful feeling to go. I needed to know all men weren't jerks.

As soon as I felt relief, I was startled when I heard Teddi's voice shout, "Hailey, what is this? Why are you kissing him like this? What is going on? Covin, the guy who took everything I wanted—why him? You're an item, and you didn't even tell me?"

Millie, not knowing anything about the situation, pulled Teddi's arm and said, "Come on, girl. It's been a long night. Let's just let them talk."

"No. I want her to talk to me. So the little note he left on our door asking to speak with you last week was because he wanted you to be his girl?"

"What's wrong with that?" Covin asked her. "I'll take care of her."

"You don't even know her," Teddi said to him.

Covin replied, "So? You don't even know me."

There had been too much drama already for me to let the two of them go at it. I took him to the side and said, "Thank you for your help tonight."

"You can't listen to her," he said. "We got something."

"I think we do, too. But understand for me that I'm gonna go back with my line sisters. I'll call you tomorrow, okay?" Though I could tell he wasn't happy, he agreed.

During the car ride home, Teddi asked a million questions. I opened my mouth not to one question. She couldn't get the hint that I didn't wanna talk about it, so I just let her vent.

Then she said, "I can't believe you're with the guy who took everything from me."

"Teddi, that guy risked his life to save yours. He gave you everything. He gave you your future. I don't know where things are going with me and Covin, but I don't have to answer to you. So many times in my life you've come first, but right now, after tonight, after everything I've been through, I wanna be happy. And if you keep getting on my nerves like this . . ."

"What? What?" she said as she hit the car window.

From the backseat, Millie said, "Calm down, Teddi. Give her some space."

"What? What? Hailey?" Teddi asked.

"You fill in the blank," I told her, tired of her riding me to see things her way.

"Time flies when you're having fun," Millie said two weeks later to me as we were in the holding room waiting for our final Gem ceremony to start.

Teddi was in the room, too, but she was over in the corner with Quisa. Evan was off to herself. She hadn't quit on us, but with G-Dogg released and none of us backing her to stay with him, she was with us but not with us. It really bothered me that our line was divided.

I wanted to hug Teddi and let her know I cared, but I didn't. A part of me wanted to say, "*Teddi, you can have Beta Gamma Pi.*" So many times I came close to telling her, "*If it weren't for me going to bat with the big sisters to get you on the line in the first place, you wouldn't even be here. Don't trip!*"

Teddi thought I was supposed to bow down to her, say I was sorry, and give up my new little romance. We timed it so neither one of us was in the room at the same time. Whoever was asleep first at night was the first one gone before the other one woke in the morning. It was actually quite childish. I hated that it seemed we acted like we couldn't stand each other.

I was about to suggest we squash all issues and be real sisters, but my thoughts were interrupted. Cassidy came to the door and said, "All right, my five Pis, line up. It's time to get one step closer to my beloved BGP."

As we walked into the room, our collegiate adviser, Dr. Weaver, was on the microphone saying, "Ladies, as you come in, reflect on the past four Gems."

And I thought back to the first one on leadership. Hayden had said that ceremony was the one that got to her the most. It *was* moving, as I was certainly motivated by what they said: work what you got and give it all you can. Reflecting on it, I realized that I was a leader, and going to my line sisters to get things straight was an area I could take the lead on.

Then I thought about Gem two on sisterhood. The basic message behind the whole thing was: The way we roll was as one unit. And if Teddi and Evan were ever to feel true love from me, I needed to give it unconditionally and be willing to work on our differences.

Gem three: act like you know. Wow! It focused on education. They said a lot of people that pledged had their GPAs go down. If you knew why you were in school, you should act like it. Do something. Be about changing your community and making your sorority better. You couldn't make it better if you had no degree. The tension my line had made all of us weaker students. We needed to fix that.

Gem four was Millie's favorite, which was Christian principles. We learned that God had it going on. Though I knew in my heart that I should treat people how I wanted to be treated, I was a little stubborn. But that hard heart needed to go. Though I was happy dating Covin, I wasn't totally okay, because I knew Teddi had issues with it.

Yep, after pondering the last two weeks, I was emotional. I'd learned how to be better, and I'd vowed to care more, yet I wasn't living up to what I'd pledged. This last Gem on public service was for me. I wasn't getting much from my line sisters, because, frankly, I hadn't given them much. And if I loved them and the bond we were supposed to be forming, why did I want anything from them anyway? Being in a sorority was not a self-serving organization.

As soon as we took our seats, Samantha said, "As far as the Gem ceremonies are concerned, you ladies have come to the end of the road. Tonight is the final Gem on public service. In this world, we are supposed to give more than we take, care about others more than ourselves, and speak for those who don't have a voice. We challenge you sitting before us who want to join our fold. Is it all about you? Or is it about your line sister? Is it about your campus? Is it about your community? Is it about your world?"

I sat there, and a tear trickled down my face. If it weren't for my mom, my sister, and Teddi's insistence, Beta Gamma Pi would have been an afterthought. Yet I was thrilled about their cause. They cared for people, and so did I.

I had forgotten how important it was to work things out with my dear friend; I could not be broken and try to fix somebody else. And as tough as I tried to act, I cared about Teddi. I didn't want Evan to be sad or alone anymore either.

As soon as the ceremony was over, I went to Teddi and Evan and said, "Forgive me. I love you both, and I'm sorry for being so distant."

Teddi replied, "I'm the one who's sorry. You're right—Covin risked his life for mine. He's a good guy who likes you. Forgive me for standing in your way."

Evan pulled up her sleeve, and we saw a big, deep bruise on her arm. She said, "You all were right. G-Dogg got out of jail, and at first things were good. Then I said something he didn't like, and I got this. I'm done, you guys. I just didn't know how to ask for help."

Millie and Quisa were standing around and heard us. We all took a few moments to be there for each other. It felt good to connect as a line.

Cassidy interrupted and ushered us out of the room. "Y'all, come on. Y'all gotta leave and go study."

Samantha came over to her and said, "What are you telling them?"

"Don't worry about it," Cassidy said to her.

"Yes, I do need to worry. I said I wanna see them right now. I'm the Chapter President, so I decide what goes on around here. If I wanna take them with another line to study, that's my business."

"Girls, y'all need to get your stuff and go study like I said," Cassidy said to us. "Now!" We picked up our stuff and headed for the door.

"I can't believe you're gonna tell them to do what you say. Y'all, I'm the Chapter President," Samantha said.

"And when other people haze these girls, you think you got control, but you don't. You don't put them around people you know are crazy."

"What, you calling me crazy now?" Samantha said as she came lunging toward Cassidy.

Cassidy went toward her. It was a horrible sight when we had just left a beautiful ceremony talking about love, oneness, and making things better. Not even five minutes later, our Chapter President and Vice President were practically at blows. Other Betas tried to help pull them apart, but they were torn down by the ladies' fists. How were we supposed to be united as sisters when our leaders' actions were way past immature and pesky?

## BASK

Sam was smiling like she wanted to throw down. "Come on, Cassidy. Show me what you got. If this is what you want, come get it."

Betas pulled them apart and yet they ran back to tear each other to shreds again. This was not ladylike behavior nor was it the Beta way to act. It was disturbing to see my big sisters act so ghetto. They were setting the wrong examples. And I knew Cassidy had more compassion than that.

"You're supposed to be our Chapter President!" Evan yelled out, not caring if it was her place or not. "Stop, please! Have some respect for yourselves and each other. I know hitting on any level is wrong."

It was weird, but I really didn't know why I wasn't more forthcoming with how awful I thought this was. I was getting mixed signals about our sisterhood. Someone needed to be the bigger person and just quit these childish antics. I looked to my line sisters, and we had to stand up with Evan. We needed to be leaders; it was time for us to step in.

Teddi said, "I ain't saying nothing. I don't want either one of them to get mad at me for taking sides, even though I think Sam is dead wrong for getting all in her girl's face."

A group of Betas took Cassidy to one side, and the others put Sam in a corner. The five of us were already on shaky ground in our own relationships, and now we were in a circle as one, wondering what our fate would be now that our leaders were at odds with each other. If this was what they considered sisterhood, did I really want to get involved deeper in this? Hayden and I argued as sisters, but not to this extent. Physical violence had never been a part of my world.

Cassidy came over to us and said, "Ladies, I apologize for what just happened. Please do not follow in my footsteps. It's time for y'all to go on your retreat. Our adviser left when the ceremony was over, and she was headed over there with some alumnae ladies. She just called, and she's wondering where you guys are. Thankfully, we can't go, or else they would see what a mess we just caused. Here's the directions."

"But we didn't bring anything for an overnight trip," Teddi said.

"You won't need anything," Cassidy responded, still clearly shaken from the fight. "Just get over there. They got you."

To ease the tension, I put my hand on her shoulder and said, "It's gonna be okay."

She gave me a small grin. Cassidy was so cool. She needed to know we cared. Sam, on the other hand, was still being calmed down by her sorors. I'd lost respect for our leader, who was unable to keep her feelings in check. And to know these two used to be roommates and best friends . . . I knew I truly needed to make sure Teddi and I got past our differences so we would not have a severe fallout like I'd just witnessed.

"Just do better than what you saw. Really talk to each other tonight and get a deeper understanding of one another. Love and respect your sister. If you got anything you wanna say, just let it out, because if you keep it in, it could blow up and get real ugly," Cassidy told us, seeing we were affected by their blowup.

The fight between Sam and her was explosive. I knew deep down she was in agony, and her bond with her sister was now broken. My line needed a retreat to make sure we reconnected.

All during the ride over to the bed-and-breakfast ten miles out from the school, I thought about Teddi. I missed my friend even before the crazy incident between Cassidy and Sam, but now that I had seen how the tightest of bonds could go to blows, I knew I needed to make sure things stayed right with Teddi. We had apologized, but we were emotional. Had we really said all we needed to say to one another?

After we had a wonderful meal with the five alumni sorors who had come to get to know and spend time with us on the retreat, we were summoned to a suite. Our charge for the evening was to really go deep.

Millie broke the awkward silence by saying, "So, anybody got something to say? We talked earlier—we're good, right?"

Quisa said, "I don't think all of us need to work on our issues; I think just two need to. Teddi and Hailey, straighten out all the tension. Evan, Millie, maybe we can walk the grounds and observe the scenery a little? We need some fresh air."

"Thanks, y'all. That would be nice," Teddi said.

I just nodded in agreement, appreciating the fact that they recognized we had some things we needed to work on, and it was private. Teddi walked our new three sisters to the door and closed it behind them. When she turned back around, I was standing, not knowing what to say.

"I am really sorry," she said, getting a little emotional. I could see the tears forming in her eyes.

"I wanted to say I'm sorry for not considering your feelings where Covin is concerned!" I said as we sat on the couch in our plush suite.

"You don't owe me an apology," Teddi said to me. "I was trying to hold you back from being with Covin, and that was wrong. I was upset with you for not telling me, and I held it in for so long. I know you got my back, front, side, everything, and I also know you bent over backward to make sure I was on this line."

I just shook my head a couple times when she said that. I swore I was gonna take that to my grave. How did she know?

"I'm not stupid," Teddi said. "I caught the vibe that the Betas weren't feeling me at first. I got a call last, after you had a meeting with them. Besides, Sam told me what you did for me during one of the Gem ceremonies. Come on, now, Hailey. I owe you so much for being so patient with me. My last two years of high school, I thought I would be nothing without my parents, but God gave me you, a best friend. I was scared that something would take you away from me. I was thinking that if you got a guy, we would lose our connection."

I grabbed my friend's hands, squeezed them tightly, and said, "I would do anything for you, girl. Don't worry about me going anywhere. Just because I have someone else in my life doesn't mean I'm going to replace you. Subconsciously, my heart has been feeling these things for a guy I've never felt before, and I wanna see where things are gonna go. It doesn't mean as much if I don't have a best friend to share it all with. Really, though, Covin is great. You may have a grudge against him for beating you in the SGA election, but I think you guys would get along great."

"I'm cool with you two dating. I know he's special to you. I can tell how you glow when you talk about him, Hailey. I'm sorry for being so petty. I promise you we will never be like Sam and Cassidy."

We hugged. Things were back in order. I just prayed that they would stay that way.

Thanksgiving had come, and my family was having a big dinner at our house. My mom told me I could invite anyone over, but Teddi was with her grandparents, Covin was with his parents, and my line sisters were with their respective families out of state. But as I looked at the feast laid out before me of turkey, collard greens, macaroni and cheese, cabbage, stuffing, potato salad, cornbread, sweet-potato pie, and red velvet cake, I realized how blessed I was, and I thought about Ms. Mayzee King's family.

I knew we were gonna have leftovers, but were they gonna have enough food? I rushed over to my mom and told her what I was thinking, and she thought it was an excellent idea to make sure the King family had food.

I didn't have their phone number, so my mom made me go over and invite them to dinner. As I stood on the front porch, waiting for someone to open the door, I smelled food. Seemed they were taken care of, but I couldn't just leave.

The kids' grandmother came to the barely stable door of the trailer. "Thank you, baby. You and your school. Y'all have just blessed me and my grandbabies so." I didn't know what she was talking about for a second. At least not until I came in and saw the card displayed on her card table from a familiar person. "That SGA President of yours, with his handsome self, came by with a bunch of groceries yesterday. Me, these grandchildren, and some of the neighbors are gonna eat all this good food."

I felt horrible that I had let Covin down. I was the director of community relations, and I didn't know anything about this. Had this pledging consumed me? Yes, it had. I hadn't been into the SGA office or with him in the last ten days. We'd had to study for our upcoming Beta test. My line had been bonding. I'd had no extra time for him. But I guessed this was his way of showing "one monkey don't stop the show." Clearly, I could see the show was doing well without me. Honestly, it was killing me.

"Why are you looking so sad, girl? Y'all helped us with so much," she said to me, confused by my reaction.

"Well, I'm glad y'all are enjoying it," I replied, looking away.

"Something's not right. Talk to me. Tell me what's wrong. You can tell me anything."

"It's nothing," I said, knowing I was here to help her, not to burden her with my issues.

"No, something's wrong," she said in a motherly tone. "Talk to me, dear."

"This was my job, and it got done without me. I feel a little bad, is all," I vulnerably admitted.

"Well, when you're a part of a team, people pick up each other's slack. That's what a family is for. Did anybody get onto you and tell you you let them down?"

"No, ma'am."

"Then do more than your part next time. You don't have to be the one who gets all the glory."

"It wasn't about me getting the glory or anything like that," I confessed. "It was about me pulling my weight."

"Well, girl, you're young. You can't be everywhere at every time. You got a good heart, and that should count for something. You came over to see about us, and I'm sure you were going to invite us to your house for dinner. A lot of people mind having poor people over to their house, but you don't. You got a good heart. What's your name, child?"

"Hailey. Hailey Grant."

"Well, Miss Hailey Grant, God is gonna bless you. Be glad He's blessing those you want to help, even if He uses someone other than you. Trust me, the Lord will use you, too," she said as we hugged. "Thanks again."

I left her house with a better understanding of my purpose on this earth. I had to understand that others care about people in need, too, and I needed to be okay with helping when I could. I had really needed that talk. She'd given much wisdom.

When I got home, my family was ready to eat. My sister was there with her boyfriend and his parents. My mom and dad seemed overly excited that they were at the table. Was there something going on I didn't know about? As long as folks were happy, I didn't need details. I was thankful.

Just when we were about to bless the food to eat, my sister's boyfriend, Creed, stood up, took Hayden's hand, and said, "I know what I'm thankful for, and that is this young lady who's been my best friend for the past four years. She's held up my strength and put up with my weaknesses. She's inspired me to be a better person. After a talk with her parents, I am excited to say, Hayden, I love you, and I can't see my life going on without you. I would like to know if you would do me the honor of being my wife." He got down on one knee, kissed her hand, and continued his proposal. "Will you marry me?"

I couldn't have been more proud when she said, "Yes, Creed."

Creed took out a ring, and the houseful of relatives, including my uncle, aunts, parents, and a host of cousins, all cheered. It was a pure, beautiful moment.

\* \* \*

The day after Thanksgiving, my mom, my sister, and I had shopped until we dropped. We were going from mall to mall, and it felt like we stopped in every store. I was exhausted. Now it was Saturday morning—time for me to sleep in and rest. They wanted to go again.

"Come on, Hailey," Hayden said. "You gotta help me prepare for my wedding."

She had just gotten engaged, and she was already set on having things lined up for her big day. I was tired; all I wanted to do was sleep in and spend some time with my dad. She and my mom could have that shopping thing. I wasn't hating or anything. It just wasn't my thing.

Then my mom cut in and said, "Please, Hailey, for me. I wouldn't have as much fun as I did yesterday without my two girls."

After she made me feel bad about not giving me that many requests and being home for the holiday, I got out of bed, threw on some sweats, brushed my teeth, and said, "All right, let's go."

"No, no, no, no," Hayden said. "You can't go anywhere like that. How about some makeup or doing something to your hair? Oh, uh-uh, Hailey. You can still see stuff on the sides of your eyes."

"It's not about me—it's about the bride. You're the one who has to try on dresses. This is your world, and I'm just a squirrel looking for a nut. I'm here only to please you," I said in the smartest tone I could muster up.

"Okay, Hailey. I understand you don't wanna go, but you're going. Just fix yourself up," Hayden replied in a bossy tone.

"Mom, will you tell her it's not that serious!" I yelled out, looking for my mom to have my side.

"Baby, it's always important to look presentable. You never know who you may run into. Now, we got a quick second, so go ahead and fix yourself. Don't take too long though."

Finally, thirty minutes later, we were in the car. I had to force myself to put on a pair of slacks and a nice shirt and pin my hair up. I wasn't too done up, but I did aim to please. I had to admit, though, I was in the backseat pouting, and all they were doing was talking about colors, flowers, and china patterns—stuff I could have been interested in if I had gotten a little more rest. I wasn't getting hazed or anything, but the sorority kept me busy. If I wasn't in class, I was busy studying for class. If I wasn't studying for classes, I was preparing for this Beta test. I practically had a twenty-four-hour day.

We were driving toward campus, and I didn't know what bridal shop was over there, but my mom and sister were so into their conversation that I couldn't get a word in to ask them where we were headed.

When we pulled up to the campus, I said, "Why are we here?"

"Oh, my brother wanted me to get something," my mom said, carefree.

I never knew her to get anything for him, but okay. As soon as we pulled up to a building—that I remembered too fondly because I had been to it so many times for Beta Gamma Pi for the past months—I started to wonder what was going on. I looked at both my mom and sister, and they were dressed in all black. Had they known something I didn't?

Hayden, sensing my confusion, said, "Don't ask any more questions, Hailey. Just get out."

I hopped out of the car and smiled from Arkansas to California. They had gotten me good. I went up to room 102, and Cassidy met me at the door. She handed me a paper and said, "Your BGP fate is in your hands. You have twenty minutes—do your best and ace the test." Why did I have only twenty minutes when the other four of my line sisters weren't even around?

When I was done, Cassidy took me to another room. There I put on a purple robe. "We have our properties now. I'll be back for you," she said as she left the room.

When the door opened again, it was Teddi. I guess I had passed my exam.

"It looks like we're crossing!" she screamed out.

"Yeah, but where are Evan, Quisa, and Millie?" As soon as I asked, the door opened again, and there they were. "I thought y'all were out of town!"

"We were going home, but we got called back. We ended up staying with our adviser," Evan said.

We were all giddy and excited. I was so fired up, overjoyed, and relieved. The Lord had spared my life this semester. Things were really looking too good for me. And I was certainly falling for Covin. These were feelings that were deep and magical. I couldn't wait to see how everything would pan out with us.

Having camaraderie with these four ladies that I admired, walking through the burning sands, having a room full of Betas—my mom and sister included—serenading us, and saying the oath that we would faithfully serve Beta Gamma Pi until the day we died was something that made me beam with pride and bask.

## GIANT

Because a lot of students didn't go home for Thanksgiving break, SGA had a party that night for those who were left at school. We found out that several other lines had crossed—the Mus and the Rhos and a couple frats. My line sisters were too excited to show off their letters. I just wanted to see Covin. I wanted so badly for him to hug me and tell me how proud he was of me that I had obtained this big feat.

When we were about to practice our new-member presentation, Teddi saw me completely distracted and said, "Sorors, our line sister Hailey needs to find her boy."

It was our night, and I didn't want to let them down if I stepped away. However, I had been putting Covin on the backburner for far too long. Needing to tend to him, I hoped my girls understood.

Evan said, "It's cool, girl. We understand."

Teddi said, "Go find him."

I positively knew we'd come a long way when Teddi wasn't stressing me to hang out with them. Don't get me wrong, I did wanna step, learn some chants, and be with my sorority sisters, but deep down I wanted to be with the guy who made my heart pitter-patter.

When I went over a little early to the place where the party was gonna be, I was happy to see Covin's car outside. Quickly, I got out and went inside. No one was on the door yet checking people to come in, so I went inside freely to look around. I called out to Covin, but I didn't see him. I went around to the back room, and he was in there with the SGA secretary, Barbie Stein. She was all smiles as he showed her the system he'd wanted to use for collecting tickets. I knocked on the door to interrupt their little meeting. I could tell, as she rolled her eyes, that it bothered her.

"What's up, stranger?" Covin said when he glanced up and saw me, letting me know he was a little irritated.

I just gave a fake smile, waiting for the girl who occupied his present time to leave, but she didn't move. Respectfully, I said, "Covin, may I speak to you for a minute?"

"Well, we're trying to get ready for this event. I got a lot of people for this SGA cabinet, but some of them have been MIA. With me trying to wear multiple hats, I don't have a lot of time."

I walked over to him. "It won't take long though. I promise."

Barbie stroked his neck and said, "Covin, you can go ahead and talk to her. I got it. Just don't stay gone too long, because we don't have much longer before we open the doors. I know we're gonna have a full house."

Then he followed me into the open spaces. He wasn't rushing into my arms. I felt bad; I'd obviously given him reason to doubt me.

"Okay, I know you are bummed with me, but there's no need for the attitude," I said, quickly trying to alleviate the drama.

"I'm just telling the truth. You signed up to help me, and you're not. You called me in the middle of the night to help you, and I was there. When I need you, you're nowhere to be found."

"What are you talking about? I didn't even know you needed me."

"I can't even leave you a message, Hailey. Your voice mail is full, and that's not good business. Why wouldn't you check in with me anyway? Lots of ideas came up for community relations, and I had to act on them myself. I didn't know what was going on with you. I thought maybe we were through."

"Oh, no," I said as I came closer to him and tried to put my hand on his face and rub it gently and calm him down. Yet he backed away really quickly and let me know I was invading his space.

"I didn't know what to think. If the shoe were on the other foot, I'm sure you would've been bummed out that you hadn't heard from me."

"I'm sorry you feel that way, Covin, and I'm sorry things have been hectic lately. I came here to let you know I crossed." I opened my jacket and showed him my Beta Gamma Pi sweatshirt.

"It's gonna be hard catering to SGA when you're serving a sorority," he said as he walked away.

"Covin, it doesn't have to be that way. There is a way I can do both."

"You know what, Hailey?" he said as he turned and faced me. "Let's not act like there's not a big elephant in the room. We know I come second to your sorority."

"I don't think I come first to SGA. You made a commitment to lead this campus."

"Yeah, and you agreed to help me."

"And I still want to. Now that the biggest part of this sorority is behind me, I'm a full-fledged member; I can dictate my own schedule. I don't have to go to mandatory things. Outside of this sorority," I said as I walked up to him, "I wanna be with you." Then I gave him a long, sweet kiss on the lips.

Moments after we connected in a special way, he said, "Well, that's what I'm talking about. I've wanted this . . . us. Glad you want us, too."

It didn't take long for sorority life to kick in full swing. It was a week later, and my line sisters and I were excited to head to our first meeting. The ceremony that had taken place at the beginning had lived up to its pomp and circumstance. Lighting the five candles in the chapter room that signified the five Gems that BGP stood for reaffirmed our vow that we were in this to make a difference.

Knowing now that we were going to respect one another, let everyone know we were going to step out there and be bold and different, and take this sorority to new heights motivated all five of us. There were about twenty-five of us in the room—my five line sisters plus the sorors from Cassidy's line who had not graduated. There was so much we were going to be able to do together.

And as soon as Sam hit the gavel, signifying that the meeting had started, a girl who hadn't been around a lot stood up and said, "I know I don't know any of you new sorors, but I'm Kim. We're still your big sisters, so I do expect you to—"

The gavel was hit a few more times, and Sam said, "You're out of line, soror. This isn't announcements."

"I don't see any agenda to follow. It is the President's responsibility to prepare an agenda. With nothing going around, you have no right to tell me if I'm in line or out of line. This is get-in-where-you-fit-in time," Kim responded.

Teddi hit me on my left leg. "I didn't know we were going to be thrown into drama."

Evan hit me on the right. "Now, they know they need to calm down and have a civilized meeting."

"I've had a heavy course load with my studies this whole semester," Kim said, "and I heard you've been bullying people, thinking you run everything around here. And I just wanna say, in front of the new sorors and to set the record straight, that this is our chapter."

Sam hit the gavel again and said, "Soror, you are out of line! And as long as the gavel is in my hands"—Cassidy whispered something in her ear—"all right, but I'm just saying she doesn't need to try me. Ladies, we were going to have an agenda, but the copy machines weren't working."

Some disrespectful sorors who didn't acknowledge Sam

were snickering. Connie, one of the sorors, blurted out, "It's not like you don't have a computer. You could've easily printed thirty to forty copies. We ain't stupid."

Cassidy was looking in the crowd to see who had said it. When she saw the confused and disheartened looks on our faces, she stood and said, "Sorors, I know everybody's probably heard about what happened between Sam and me."

"Yeah, and she owes you an apology," Kim stood up and said.

Sam hit the gavel again. "Okay, I'll apologize publicly. Cassidy and I have talked, and we're working on our issues, but to make y'all feel better, as your President I should have kept my cool. Now, we are trying to conduct business here, and we need to calm down and not be hot under the collar."

"Are you trying to say I'm hot under the collar?" Kim yelled out. "This isn't just your chapter, Sam. Cassidy may be cool with you, but most of us are not. You've changed since we elected you. And you need to be held accountable."

"For real, don't get it twisted. You're the president, not a dictator, and you can't scare me into letting you walk all over me," Connie said.

Sam got up and looked liked she wanted to stomp all over Connie. It was madness. Folks were pulling Connie back and she was walking to the front. Obviously she was ready to take on Sam, if it came to that. Sam then shook her head and sat down.

"Kim and Connie, everyone can have an opinion," Sam said, actually calming herself. "Now is not the forum to

express it. Let's talk offline. Right now we need to be re-
spectful to the process. Besides, we have the neos here for
the first time, and we all have to respect each other. And
you guys will respect that I'm your President, and today I
want to talk about what kind of service project or fund-
raiser we can do to bring some extra money in here. To
begin, no dances. SGA has taken that away from the
Greeks, as they practically do one every other day, it seems
like. Any suggestions?"

No one was throwing any ideas out there, so I raised
my hand and said, "What about a Mr. Beta Gamma Pi
contest, where the contestants are guys on our campus?
They do a talent and show off their bodies, and some of
the money would go toward scholarships for them and
the other money we keep for our public service project.
We can help Ms. King's family who is struggling."

A lot of people started clapping and commenting on
how they thought that was a good idea. I was happy the
concept was well received. Some sorors were hitting me
on the back, and I didn't feel I deserved all that. I was
throwing out ideas, just doing my part.

When the noise got a little out of hand, Sam hit the
gavel and said, "All those in favor of a Mr. Beta Gamma
Pi contest, say aye." The room was full with ayes, and no
one opposed. "Great. We got ourselves a contest. And,
Hailey Grant, I want you to chair it."

I got so many grunts and mumbles. Some sorors were
saying I was too new to chair. I hated that she'd asked me
to do it, but it seemed like no one else could work with
Sam. And it was my idea. Though I had a lot on my plate
already, I was up for the challenge. I couldn't wait to step

up and prove people wrong. I would show them that they could work with me, and everything would work out great.

The semester had been flying by, and there was lots of buzz about our contest. We had forty-two applications, interviewed thirty-two handsome men, and narrowed it down to the top twenty guys we wanted to represent our sorority in the contest. They were leaders, had big dreams, spoke extremely well, and, oh, did I mention they were fine?

There had been a lot of talk going around the chapter about people not thinking I would be able to handle the job. I wasn't surprised when my line sisters were a part of that conversation. We'd said during our pledge time that we'd tell each other about issues so nothing could fester.

I got tired of overhearing bits and pieces of their negative conversations one day. So I called them to the side and said, "Look, what's up with the lack of support? Anyone has a problem with me, let's talk. I expect different from my sands. I'm not saying this is going to be perfect, but I definitely need y'all's support. I need y'all to help me make sure that I don't fail. If our big sisters had any other ideas that were better and could do this without us, they would've come up with an idea, or they would have already been doing something major. It's time for us to hit the ground running. Our line name isn't called Essence in Distinction for nothing. We've got class and camaraderie. Don't make their side conversations turn us into catty women." They all seemed to take in what I said and agreed.

Teddi said, "Seems we let the green-eyed monster get the best of us. And, yep, big sisters have been putting negative things in our ears, like why did Sam choose you over us, and we tripped. But no more. Let's meet with these guys as one unit. Hailey, you're leading the effort, and this event will be successful."

This was the first meeting we had for our contestants. This was the first time we would see them all together, and we were gonna have a dynamic show. Women were going to pack the place. We just knew it because all the male studs had it going on.

There was this one guy who kept smiling at me. Morgan Brunette was six-four with dark honey, mocha-chocolate skin and muscles bulging out of his sweater. His deep stare made me melt.

It was actually hard for me to concentrate on what I was doing because every time I passed his way, giving out information and collecting forms they needed to submit, he touched me. I looked over to the left, and I saw my sands whispering about him, too. Something about him was mesmerizing and could set a girl on fire. And this Brunette dude was certainly doing this to me. Every woman in here knew I had a guy, one who truly was Mr. Right. Why was I eyeing another?

"Okay, I want to call you guys' attention to the paper before you. As you see, the contest will be held the last month of school. We'll be meeting weekly when we come back off from Christmas break. We are asking you all to raise a minimum of five hundred. If you do, you'll receive forty percent, and anything over the five hundred you raise, you'll get sixty percent. In addition to fund-raising, you'll also be responsible for talent and modeling. There will be judges to judge your presentations and decide who Mr. Beta Gamma Pi is. And if you have any more questions . . ." I paused.

Morgan cunningly asked, "If we have any more questions, can we come see you? I need an address or phone number so I can reach you." He was flirting.

And consciously flirting back, I said, "You'll see on the page at the bottom that I gave y'all my phone number. If you need to use it . . . use it." And then I shrugged my shoulders.

The guys had some other questions, and I answered them. As soon as we were adjourned, Morgan made his way toward me. I was only five feet, six inches, and he towered over me, but it wasn't an eerie hovering. It was one that made me feel safe, like he was about to wrap his tight and chiseled arms around me.

He looked deep into my eyes and said, "I will certainly be giving you a call."

Then he bent over and planted a long kiss on my cheek. When he walked away I wanted to scream, but everyone in the room could see I was fascinated with the giant.

## PINCH

*W*hen Morgan turned around, came back toward me, brushed up against my chest, and reached for the papers he'd laid on the desk when he kissed me, I was caught between a rock and a hard place. My heart was beating, and my line sisters were furious. I could tell. They weren't looking directly at me, but I knew they were not happy at all.

Morgan said, "I forgot this. I was so excited to get your number I forgot the information. That wouldn't do us any good, huh? Seeing as y'all need us to raise a lot of money for charity and us dudes need to raise money for tuition."

Licking my lips, I couldn't respond. This guy was just a man's man. Rough, unpolished, yet so together. It was scary.

As soon as he left for the final time, Teddi came over to

me, tugged my arm, and said, "Hailey, why don't you just take off your panties in front of him already?"

"What are you talking about?" I said to her, trying to play it off. "He needed his information."

"Girl, Morgan Burnette has a helluva rep. Don't get caught in the good looks," Teddi scolded.

The other three of my line sisters ganged up and were on Teddi's side. Evan and I had been connecting. She was really trying to forget G-Dogg, and he'd been calling. Every time she got the urge to return his advances, she called me. So I knew she would have my back. That theory was quickly shot to the moon when she said, "Yeah, you were a little too giddy. 'Are you sure you're going to call me?'" she mocked.

"Hailey, I'm just saying," Millie said in her mouse voice, "you're the chair of this event, and you're not supposed to mix business with pleasure. From what I just witnessed, everything was way too hot. It was almost X-rated."

"You guys are so tripping. Y'all were snickering and grinning over him as well."

Quisa said, "Yeah, we were checking him out, and the brother is fine, but none of us has a boyfriend. And as was just brought to your attention, we're not the chair."

"What does me being the chair have to do with anything? Are you insinuating that I'm mixing business with pleasure? Okay, listen up. We are all in college, okay? And though I have a boyfriend, there is no ring on my finger," I said, dangling my hand in their faces.

"Oh, come on," Teddi said to me. "Hailey, you and I fell out at the top of the school year because you were so into our new SGA President. What, y'all broke up or something?"

"No! I'm meeting up with him later on. Everything is fine. You guys are overreacting. You saw a little playful fun with me and a contestant. You gotta work with what you got."

"Yeah, but you also gotta represent yourself the right way. Ain't no need in giving away false signals. The way you were hanging on was a little sleazy, definitely not Beta Gamma Pi material," Teddi said to me, crushing my heart.

"Okay, you're really overreacting, and I'm a little offended that you practically called me a slut."

"I'm not calling you a slut. I'm saying you were acting slutty. You were so into it you can't even see how you schmoozing up to him came across. Even just then when he brushed up against you, you were acting like it was one hundred and fifty degrees."

"Okay!" Evan said, agreeing with Teddi. "Yeah, it was too hot up in here."

Teddi said, "Bottom line, Hailey, just stay away from the guy. You got a good thing going on with Covin. Your passion should be burning like that for him. Don't let this boy you barely know come and douse water on your blossoming relationship."

Quisa chimed in and said, "Yeah. Morgan is the kind of guy you bang, and Covin is the type you keep. You're the type who can't play both of them. So get your feelings in check now."

"We're saying this because we love you," Teddi said. "I

backed off being mad about you and Covin because I knew deep down he'd do right by you. But this slick trick . . . I don't think so. Don't be no fool."

Tired of hearing my new mommies dictate my life, I grabbed my stuff and stepped outside the door. I was fuming mad. In the back of my mind, I was wondering were they right? Was I tripping? Was I having fun? Or was I messing up a good thing?

"You didn't have to cook for me," I said to Covin as I sat at the table in his new apartment.

Since the fire, his dad had been putting pressure on him to move off campus. This was tough for him because he liked being connected to the students on a more personal level, but he had finally given in. And I had to admit his pops had set him out. Covin had a really nice pad. It was a one-bedroom, one-and-a-half-bath decked out in colors for a king—purple and gold. The full bathroom with a whirlpool tub was attached to his room. He had a huge kitchen engulfed by a nice-sized dining area. Incense and candles had his place smelling good. There was ambiance in the air. Off the bat, I was a tad uncomfortable.

"I know I didn't have to," he said as he handed me flowers and kissed me on the cheek, "but I wanted to. Dinner will be ready in just a sec, so why won't you relax and talk to me while I fix my baby a meal?"

He was getting overly comfortable with me. We had decided to date and all, and don't get me wrong, I liked him, but I could see where this night was headed. I was no fool. Luther playing in the background. Aromatherapy candles lit all around to set the mood. Neither one of us was twenty-one years old, but there was a bottle of wine on the table as well. I wasn't sure if he'd sprayed Febreze, had plug-ins, or what, but the place smelled great!

"You looked around—you like what you see in here?" he asked, alluding to himself.

Trying not to stroke him, I said, "Yes. It's very nice in here."

"I've been trying to get you over for a couple days to have a woman's touch to make this place nice, but you were busy."

"Yeah, I'm chair of this project and—"

"I don't wanna talk about sorority stuff," he said as he turned the stove down low, came over to me, and kissed me on the neck. "I want tonight to be strictly about us. How can we get closer? How can we take this to the next level? I feel a little disconnected to you. I see you only in my dreams, never in reality anymore. We're both going in opposite directions, but tonight is totally about us."

He started kissing on my neck again. I didn't want to pull away. I didn't want him to think I wasn't down for what he was saying, but in reality I wasn't sure if I was down.

"Babe, I'm hungry," I said to him, sliding away just a little, but not so abruptly that he would get upset.

"Yeah, we can get back to this after dinner. Babe, I want you to try this sauce I made."

"Spaghetti!" I said excitedly.

"Yeah, I did a lil' something."

He had angel-hair pasta tossed in Italian dressing with hamburger and Italian sausage marinated in mushroom sauce. It was a little sweet with garlic bread and salad.

Everything was delicious! I tried to make the moment stretch because I could tell by the way he was looking at me that he wanted to get me in the next room. And I didn't wanna give off any signals that I was down for that.

"You seem distant," he said to me as he took my plate.

"No, I'm just a little tired. So tell me about SGA—what do you need me to do now?"

"I need you not to focus on work, school, or anything else other than us. Can you do that for me?" he asked as he pulled me over to the couch. Before I knew it he had taken off my shoes and was rubbing my feet.

"Your feet are beautiful," he whispered to me, licking his lips like he was ready to suck them.

I moved his mouth up but allowed him to give me a massage. It did feel relaxing, but I wasn't trying to give him mixed signals. So, finally, I stood and said, "We need to talk."

"You've got to be kidding me. You're gonna stop the mood to tell me that. We can talk later. I'm sure whatever it is can wait. Let's let our bodies do the talking."

"I just think we're moving too fast," I said as he worked his way up my body with his hands. "Maybe we should see other people," I blurted out.

"What?" he said, completely freaked out. "Hailey, if that's what you want, I'll have to respect that and give you space."

A tad pissed, he abruptly blew out the candles on the table and turned on the lights. "You can go. Dinner's done." Covin walked into his bedroom and closed the door behind him.

I walked to the front door and let myself out. As I stood on the other side of the door, I wondered if I had made the biggest mistake of my life or if I had missed out on a mistake by not sleeping with Covin when I wasn't ready. I was confused, but I was young. I felt like I was in a jam. I had made my decision, and it was time for me to get to the core of what I was thinking. *Morgan Brunette, right or wrong, here I come.*

"I honestly didn't think you were going to go out with me," Morgan said a few days later as I rode with him in his car to a club.

I just sorta smiled and then looked out the dark, cloudy window. "Do you even think it's a good idea to go out tonight?" I said to him, knowing a severe storm was supposed to hit the state.

"They did say we were gonna have a little thunderstorm come our way. Or was it a tornado watch? I don't remember. You said yes, girl—I was not gonna let you stay inside because of a little rain," he said as he touched my leg and sent chills all over my body. Then he touched my chin and said, "All right. Tell a brother why it took so long for you to say yes. I knew you wanted to be with me."

He was so cocky, but he was so dead-on. I wanted to be with him, and he knew it. But a part of me knew it was wrong. I was usually a sensible person. Wouldn't go outside without a coat or a jacket in the fall. Would finish all my homework before I had fun. I never imagined myself wanting to be with the bad boy, but here I was, caught up. His touches got to me way more than Covin's did.

All my life I'd been good, and maybe I had to learn for myself that walking on the wild side of life was dangerous. But like I often used to think about girls who made stupid decisions, you couldn't tell me to stay away from the stove if the burner was on high. Being with Morgan made me feel invincible; there was no way I could get burned.

I just sorta looked at him, checking out his lips, wishing they were touching mine, digging his hands, imagining they were all over me, and wondering what was between his . . . Well, I don't need to finish that thought, do I?

"You're thinking something over there—what's up? Ask me whatever's on your mind."

I paused before I responded. "Okay, at the contestants' meeting last week, all my sorority sisters are cute and got it going on, but you were looking at me. I just wondered—"

He chuckled. "Why I picked you? Well"—he reached over, grabbed my hand, and placed it between his legs— "you're over the whole contest, you present so well, you walk around and all us guys were checking you out, and—"

"Oh, so it's a competition thing?" I asked, cutting him off.

"No, it's not. It was turning me on that other people were into you, too. I'm the kinda guy that likes people to get things for themselves, but if I see something I want, I'm gonna go for it. I had no problem letting you know I was interested. Plus, I knew I'd like your touch. You gave me an inch—"

"So you took a mile," I said, finishing his statement and removing my hand.

"Yeah, are you mad?"

"I wouldn't be out with you if I were."

"Exactly what I'd hope to hear you say," he said.

I wasn't trying to compare Morgan to Covin, but I must admit they were extremely different. Morgan was steamy, but Covin was dreamy. You know girls dreamed of having a gentleman, but they long to be seduced, too.

When we pulled up to the restaurant, he got out of the car first, and I waited for him to open my door. Good thing I wasn't holding my breath while I waited because I would've died!

When we got to the door of the restaurant, he walked in and shut the door in my face. I was a little irritated. I had to be honest with myself: did I really want to be with a guy who didn't open the door for me? Though it was a little thing, little things could go a long way.

I stood there and waited for him to come back and open it. He returned and said, "Wait. You're not one of those kind of girls, are you? I just told you I liked that you were strong. I don't need to open doors for you."

"Yeah, but I like my man stronger." I wanted to say, "You are paying for the date tonight, right?"

There were only a couple people in the restaurant. As soon as we stepped inside, he ordered a beer. I wasn't opposed to drinking, but I guess I wasn't for it either. Really, it didn't matter to me at this point. I wanted to spend some time with him and get to know him better. If he seemed to be too intoxicated, that would be out.

"Come on, let's dance. I want you to sex me up," he

said as he grabbed my hand and pulled me onto the dance floor, grabbing my behind a little too hard. Yeah, he was attractive, but I wasn't feeling him at this moment.

Across the room, a violent brawl broke out. I looked really hard, and it was G-Dogg. I knew Evan's guy was no good. No good for her or any other girl, for that matter. He was pointing a 9mm at the chest of another dude who was wearing a black bandanna. This scene had gang activity written all over it.

G-Dogg took the gun from the other guy's chest and aimed it in the air, shooting three rounds. Everyone panicked, and there was pure pandemonium as people tried to exit the building. When I turned around to tell my dude we needed to leave, he was nowhere in sight! I was terrified, alone, and in a serious pinch.

# BLACKBERRY

$\mathcal{M}$y phone started losing it as several text messages came across. *Where are you?* one read. Another had *Are you safe?* The last had *A tornado has just hit a town near us.* I read them so quickly I didn't even see who they were from.

But as people ran around crazily, I was in my own whirlwind. I had no time to answer anyone because I needed to make sure my butt didn't get shot. Someone came by and pushed me, which it threw my phone across the room. When I tried to go get it, gunshots were returned by the rival gang. As I ducked, glass at the bar was shattered and sprawled on me, cutting me in my brow. Most people were gone, but about a dozen of us were caught in the severe cross fire.

The club manager frantically screamed out, "They're

blocking the exits! We've all gotta go toward the kitchen to the freezer! Come on, let's go! Let's go!"

I had no idea where Morgan was, but, luckily, I grabbed my phone and saw it had a message from my parents. They were worried and hadn't heard from me. This wasn't even tornado season. It was December, for goodness' sake. Though it wasn't the season, the weather had a mind of its own because there was definitely a tornado in our state. As though the turmoil from the fighting weren't enough, the howling winds, falling debris, severe rain, and thunder were scaring me to death as well.

"The chair is on top of me—I can't move! Miss, help me, please!" a voice called out to me as I was running in the direction of everyone else left in the club. I didn't even know how I heard the voice. There was so much noise from the terrible weather and gangs' trash talking.

It was a man behind the bar, and an enormous piece of glass from the mirror had fallen and was stuck in his leg. I didn't have time to waste. It was more than obvious that there was no way I would be able to lift the large object out. Time was running out fast. At that very moment, the roof was being torn off the building.

The club manager saw me looking over the bar, not understanding what was going on, and called out, "Miss, come now! We're gonna lock this door to keep the thugs out. They can kill each other, but I ain't dying because of their senseless feud. We have to move toward the area that's insulated till the cops get here and stop this foolishness."

"Sir, there's a man trapped over here. I think he's your

bartender. His leg is gashed open from the mirror debris. I can't lift him. You gotta come save him."

"Oh, no, that's Mark!" the manager called out before turning toward the other people in the refrigerator. "Are there any other young men who can lend me a hand?"

I walked closer to the door and saw seven scared folks. I was stunned to see big ole Morgan as one of them. I pointed and said, "That's my date. I'm sure he can help."

Morgan came from the back of the tight, cold room and said, "Don't go volunteering me for nothing. That's how brothers die—try to start a fight or stop one. I am not a fool. I'm walking far away from the drama. Almost made it out the door till one of them guys locked it."

"No one is asking you to stop anything. Someone out there needs help. The bartender is seriously hurt. You gotta help!" I pleaded.

"Please, you know the old saying—all I gotta do is stay black and die. I don't plan to do that tonight. I ain't stepping out into that. Bullets have no names on them."

I understood what he was saying, but someone had risked her life to save mine. If Ms. Mayzee had thought like him, I would not be here myself. I had to care. My cruel stare told Morgan how disappointed I was in him.

He said, "Look, I'm glad you got in here. We need to keep this door closed to keep the fighting out there. People said they're fighting over drug money. That means they gon' be in there till only one person is standing. We don't need to be up in that. The police will come, and they'll want witnesses. They'll kill you so you can't talk. If you and the manager go out there, none of us will be safe."

I couldn't believe what he was saying! There was a man out there who needed our help. And though it was risky, how could I think about not doing everything I could to save him? And if I perished in my efforts, then it was just my time. But Morgan stayed strong and would not move.

The manager heard the groans from the injured Mark and said, "Is anyone else willing to help me?"

I was ready to move and help lift Mark myself, but two other male customers stood, and the manager told me I'd helped enough. As they went into the nonstop debris blood bath, I prayed. I felt Morgan breathing deeply behind me, but he was the last person I wanted to entertain.

Morgan grabbed my hand in his. "Okay, now, he'll be okay. We need to get inside this freezer."

I pulled away from him as hard as I could and said, "You got your way. You ensured you saved yourself. I'm waiting by this door to open it as soon as they come this way with him."

"You stay by this door, and you won't be alive. Sometimes you have to cut your losses and move on."

"If you stand here to save yourself and not risk helping someone else, I don't know how you can live with it. I'd go outta my mind if I were you. I'm not saying I got nine lives, but just this year God has taught me you gotta care about people and help when you can."

"Yeah, you can pray for people, but you have to be safe," Morgan argued, flicking his hand at me like he was tired of trying to convince me he was right as he went to the back of the freezer.

Moments later, the three men came to the back with

Mark. His leg was completely bloody and still had a shard of glass in it, but they did make it back. We wrapped part of his leg with a tablecloth. We all stayed there, hoping the police would come and that the town was still intact.

I tucked my head between my legs and prayed. *Lord, please help us get through this. Help everyone who's out there. I know You have a time for us all, but thank You for giving me present life. Thank You for giving me a heart big and massive enough to care about others and want to help them more than myself. And thank You for helping me see that Morgan is not the right one for me. The arms I longed to be in all night are unequally yoked from mine. I mean, he's thinking about everything other than pleasing You. And I know You call us to be linked with people who have the same beliefs. I feel good resting in Your cozy arms, Jesus. Ms. Mayzee gave her life to save mine. I couldn't live with myself if I didn't do the same.*

My phone vibrated loudly and uncontrollably. It was my mom. Her text read *Please tell me you're okay, Hailey.* I was happy to text back *Mom, I'm fine.* I wisely told her what she wanted to hear. I didn't want her to know I wasn't okay.

My heart was light and relieved when the cops busted into the club. We heard the gunshots cease, and the manager made sure it was okay for us to go out into the once hopping place. We gave statements and our information to the police in case we needed to be questioned again. Thankfully, no one was dead—just tons of injured guys on both sides. The ambulances came, and we made sure Mark got attention quickly.

G-Dogg saw me leaving. "Shorty, I ain't know you was here. I'ma be gone for good bit this time, fo' sure. Take care of Evan for me. Got it?"

The policeman tightened up the handcuffs, and G-Dogg would not walk away, seemingly waiting on my answer. I nodded. I owed the thug nothing, but I knew I already was going to do what he asked. Evan was gonna be okay. I was going to make sure of it.

I guess I was blessed to have so many people care about me. After I sent my mom a text, my phone continued to blow up. My blood sister, Hayden; my line sisters; the dean of pledges; and a shocking text from Covin: *Just wanted to make sure you're cool.*

*What are you doing, Hailey?* I had thought to myself while I was in the back of the freezer. The others who had been in the cold place with me and Morgan at the time were now hugging, embracing, saying how much they cared about each other. And I knew there was nothing of substance between Morgan and myself, and as I looked down at my phone, I also knew I should have been out on a date with someone who really cared about me. Someone who cared about the well-being of others just like I did. Someone who didn't mind getting a little dusty or even bruised black and blue to help people. Someone excited to stand for something bigger than themself.

"You can have an attitude all you want, but we need to go home," Morgan said to me as I looked at him like I wanted to pick up one of the weapons—now on a table collected by the detectives—and use it on him.

"You're right, I can have an attitude, and I am deserving of feeling this way toward you. In my eyes you may have muscles bulging everywhere, but you're worse than the lion in *The Wizard of Oz*. You're a coward."

"Whatever, Hailey. Like on an airplane, don't put the mask on somebody else before you put it on yourself. I had to make sure I was safe. I tried to make sure you were straight, too, but when you wanted to watch the door, you were on your own. I give a lot, but there's gotta be something in it for me."

"Wow. Well, listen to that. If you truly give, you're not giving—you're trading," I said to him as I thought about a philosophy my dad had told me that he'd learned in the Navy.

Huffing and puffing, Morgan thought he was doing me a favor by asking, "Well, I'm leaving. Do you want a ride or not?"

"Miss, what school do you attend?" asked a man who had helped the manager with his wife standing next to him.

"Western Smith College, sir," I responded, rolling my eyes for Morgan to leave me alone.

"We'll be swinging past there. We can give you a ride if you want," the patron's wife said to me.

"Thank you," I said, gladly taking them up on the offer; riding with strangers who were heroic was much better than being with a dude I now knew to be a jerk.

Walking out, Mark, the guy I'd risked my life to help— called out from the back of the ambulance. "You just don't know what a blessing you are! Most people would've been like that guy you were with, just happy to save themselves." And then he started crying. "I guess I gotta call you a hero."

"No, you don't have to do anything but get to the hospital and treat that leg. Pay it forward, as the saying goes. Somebody saved my life, and I'm happy to make sure yours was safe, too." Then we shook hands.

The club manager said, "I'm Jim. In all the commotion, I forgot to introduce myself. When we get this place back up and running, you gotta come back with some of your girls and have a drink on me."

I nodded. We all finally looked around and noticed that outside was a bit of a mess. The storm had been merciful; buildings in our town held up, but the devastating scene was indescribable. Trees were down. Roofs were off. People had outages and visible damage. As I arrived back at school, I learned that, thankfully, all of our buildings stood tall, and everybody was accounted for. Teddi was the first to come hug me.

"Girl, where have you been? We all were so worried."

"It's a long story I have to tell you over warm blankets, fresh cookies, and hot tea."

I told my girl, and I cried in her arms. I'd been such a fool, and Teddi was kind enough not to say, "I'd told you so." She also encouraged me, saying I hadn't lost all my marbles because at least I was done with Morgan. That I was.

"There's an SGA phone-tree message going around. They want us to go to a trailer park in the next county to clean up some of the debris," Teddi informed me, seeing I was melancholy. "You up to helping? It's a mess. I'm headed out now."

Without hesitation, I put on sweats and joined her for the road trip. I still hadn't answered Covin's text. He wasn't in the group going to the trailer park. Probably just as well I didn't see him.

It was five AM, and the light was just cracking through the sky. As we neared the town of Conway, Arkansas, I pepped up. As I looked around at the town that had lost nearly everything, I was quickly reminded of how blessed I was. I still had a lot.

When the Western Smith caravan got to the trailer park that was destroyed, I was just pleased entirely to help out where I could. We were here to help anyone try to collect the things they could salvage. Then I came across the cop whose face I would never forget—he had badly beat up G-Dogg. He was sitting in the middle of wreckage, looking like he was wondering what he was going to do next. As angry as I had been that day at his actions, I felt his heart was now broken, and it broke my own heart.

As I studied the movement of folks helping, I realized these people were still blessed as well. They had something many never get: they had each other.

I went over to him, placed my hand on his shoulder, and said, "Sir, I don't know if you remember me, but . . ."

He looked up and said, "Yeah, I know your face. You're from Western Smith. Thanks for helping us. Since I was suspended, I've realized I was wrong."

"You weren't wrong about the guy's bad character. He's in jail again. It just was too much," I said honestly, looking at both sides.

"No one deserves brutality. I'm sure feeling it now," the cop said.

"I am so sorry about all this. But I do want to help. I can only imagine how devastating this is. But all is not lost. You got a community you can lean on to help you get through this turmoil."

Others would've turned their cheeks if they knew he was a racist cop. But it wasn't about who was racist or who wasn't. It wasn't about harboring or holding grudges. It was about being better, being a part of change and wanting to get along to make our state better in the midst of tragedy. Maybe the good that had come out of this was that we could now possibly heal quickly. I sure was trying to.

I was so happy to usher in a new year. I actually wished I could close my eyes and make my whole sophomore year of college to start over. But as that wasn't possible, hopefully, my New Year's resolution of just being thankful and not taking anything for granted would allow me to have peace. I mean, how could I not be thankful? God had spared my life from a fire and allowed me to stop a cop's attack, and I'd survived not getting shot in a club where pandemonium had rung out. But in all three incidents, it wasn't like I had come away completely unscathed. I had witnessed tragedy.

Ms. Mayzee was dead. Her mom was now raising three little ones with barely a dime. Because being an attorney was something I was thinking seriously about, I had been closely following the prosecution of G-Dogg and all the boys who had shot up the club, as well as the civil suits against the cops. In the latter situation, people were going to lose their jobs. During the tornado, the town of Conway had lost homes and five people, and people's personal prized possessions were also gone. On top of all that, I had made a bad decision and let Covin go. I had told him we needed time apart so I could sow my wild oats. And, boy, did the oats sow me.

Morgan dropped out of the contest, and so did nine other participants, so we were now down to ten. The chapter sorors who thought I couldn't do it talked about me instead of rallying around to help me find other contestants or make sure the ones we had were successful. I only had my line sisters to count on. As I stood at a rally I had put together myself for the campus and community to honor Dr. Martin Luther King, Jr., I heard Covin speak, and I was inspired.

"You see, nowadays we have cell phones, computers, and e-mail to do all this communication, and some of us still don't answer the call. Back in the 1960s, there was a man who stood up for what he believed in. He gave his life so we could live better. It doesn't matter if you think life isn't fair—don't crawl under a rock, don't take the path of least resistance, and don't try to save yourself without taking a page from this man's phenomenal life. If not you, then who? If you don't help someone succeed, who's gonna save you from falling? We are Western Smith College, and we are tomorrow's future. We have no excuses. We can change the world."

Covin was so strong, and it wasn't only because he was saying powerful things but because you could tell from his demeanor and his presence and from the way the crowd was listening to him that he really believed those things. I already knew I had messed up things between us. But just watching him up there doing his thing and motivating a group of unmoved and tired college students made me wish I had him back. Yet I had made my bed. Now I could clearly see how great he was. I was the dummy who had let him go; I knew I didn't deserve him.

Covin continued. "So as we remember a great leader who paved the way for us all, let us leave from this place and not let his life, legacy, and love for us, his people, go in vain. If I have to remind you every day, for those of you who signed up to be on the SGA e-mail, I will stay on you like white on rice and tell you all you can do it, you can make a difference, and you are a leader. And I'll do it. It's so easy to press one button to send you all a challenging message from my BlackBerry."

# GOSH

Being the chair for the Mr. Beta Gamma Pi contest was a lot to deal with. I was responsible for a budget. I had to oversee cochairs and subcommittee chairs. I had to make sure minutes for our meetings were taken so we'd have a record of all decisions. More than anything, I guess the thing I found the hardest to balance was managing the different personalities.

"Okay, I just wanna know why our big sisters are at our meeting when they haven't been here for the past three weeks?" Teddi said to me, Evan, Millie, and Quisa as five of the prophytes walked through the door.

Connie, the one who along with her friend, Kim, challenged the Chapter President not too long ago, said, "What are y'all looking at? What, y'all think we can't come to any of the meetings?"

"Well, you haven't been to any of the others," Evan

said, finding her strong voice now that she was thankfully completely out of love with G-Dogg.

"We're here now, so that's all that matters," Connie said. "We've been hearing the contestants have been dropping out, and nobody has sold hardly any tickets to the event. Y'all got less than three months to pull it off, and it seems like you need our help."

Under her breath, Teddi said, "We really don't need your help."

"I don't know which one of you said something smart, but just to let you know, a Beta can be on any committee at any time," Connie said.

"No, no, we'll be glad for you to help," I said, looking at my line sisters harshly.

I motioned for the prophytes to take a seat so we could begin. "Evan, as chair over the participants, could you please give your report at this time?"

"Yes. I'll start with the contestants. Just so you know, we are down to ten, but I'd rather have ten hardworking brothers put their best feet forward than twenty only worried about how they'll look on the runway, you know?" My line sisters shook their heads to agree. Clearly, the other half of the room didn't buy it—they had pasted frowns on their faces.

Immediately, Connie raised her hand. I acknowledged her as chair, and she said, "Can we go out and solicit some more guys? Ten people puts us way under the projected amount we were looking to get. In order for us to maintain a healthy profit, each guy is pretty much going to have to double what they were supposed to bring in. And isn't that a little unrealistic? We're Betas. We know tons of guys, and they all want to be around us."

"Yeah, but we're not going to be adding people just to add them," Evan said, standing her ground. "It was hard to find ten at this stage in the competition. It wouldn't be fair to the ten who remained if we just let people come on."

"At this point, we're not in this to be fair, we're here to make a profit," Connie retorted.

Evan looked at me like *Speak up! Chime in!* It seemed like I was being hazed by the prophytes—"You better not say anything against what we believe." So we moved on to Quisa's section.

After getting the cue from me, Quisa said, "The guys will be modeling formalwear, casualwear, and sporty attire. This section will be very critical for the young men competing to represent us as Mr. BGP."

Erica, a sassy, shorthaired girl I didn't know that well, said, "So we're not doing a swimsuit competition?"

Quisa said, "No, we thought we'd keep it more professional."

Erica said, "Girl, we're a well-known college campus. It's not like they're gonna be nude! That's exactly why y'all not selling any tickets. If they showed some skin, this place would be packed."

"We all voted a while back, and we told the guys they would not be wearing swimsuits," Quisa said.

"Well, let's revote so you can untell them," Erica said, standing to her feet.

"I'm not untelling them anything," Quisa said as she stood, too.

This just became a back-and-forth argument over the swimsuits.

Teddi went on to give her report about finances, and it was completely bleak. We hadn't come anywhere close to reaching the goal we wanted for ticket sales or for the money the guys were raising.

Connie threw up her hands and said, "I don't even know why you guys are in charge of this. We're going to talk to the President. Y'all need to let us take over and run this. Just because you had a good idea doesn't make you a good chair."

She looked at me, rolled her eyes, and walked out of the room. My heart was crushed. I'd been giving this project my all. Honestly, after this divisive meeting, my all wasn't enough. Dang.

As soon as the prophytes left, Evan came over to me and said, "Oh, you're just gonna let them run the meeting? You could've had our back, Hailey."

Quisa, not wanting to add to my stress as I sank in the chair, said, "I know they come off like they own everything and we're incompetent, but we gotta stick together. And you should've told them it was what it was, and if they wanted to join us, fine, but we weren't going to change the program to please them. By you saying nothing, I don't know, it was like you weren't pleased with our plans either."

Teddi was over in the corner huffing. Finally, she came over to me and said, "Is that the case, Hailey? Are you not feeling where we are with this program thus far?"

"Won't you guys back up and give her some space?"

Millie said. "Y'all are drilling her like the prophytes were. We're supposed to have each other's back, not throw drama in your sister's face."

"That's what we're saying. You should've had our backs, Hailey," Teddi said. "Tell us where you stand with this."

I knew I needed to respond. I had been quiet for too long. But in the end, I didn't want to hurt my girls' feelings. Maybe we really couldn't do it alone, and we needed a little extra push. It was time to take charge like I had when we first met with the contestants—time to be a leader over my sands.

I said to them, "I do think they could've been here all along, but you know they were so salty at first because Sam gave us the responsibility to carry out this event. Maybe we are overwhelmed. Contestants have dropped out. We're losing money. It was said a couple days ago if we don't sell these tickets and don't raise this money, we'll be working hard for nothing almost. So if our sorors can come on board and give us ideas, maybe we can get better results."

"They weren't trying to give us ideas. They were basically scrapping everything we had, throwing it out the window and forcing us to start over!" Teddi screamed. "If they come back, I'm quitting."

She and Evan were tuned in with each other on this as Evan joined Teddi's side and said, "Yeah, me, too."

"I'll quit, too," Quisa said.

I just looked to Millie like *Help me!* There was no way I could do this program without them. They had all been making inroads I wasn't in on. I didn't keep up with every detail, because we were a team.

"Y'all, we can't quit," Millie said. However, her soft words made no impact on none of them.

I got up and jogged out of the room. "Connie!" I yelled out. "Could y'all come back here, please?"

"For what?" she called back.

"Please just come back. It's important," I said, pleading to make a difference.

"Oh, no! You're gonna call them back in here after we protested to quit? Hailey, you've lost all your cool points with us," Teddi said as she headed toward the same door through which I hoped Connie would enter.

"Y'all aren't going anywhere," I said to Teddi, finally putting my foot down as I blocked her exit.

After short moments, I had both sides back in the room. "Okay, I guess I wanna start by saying I appreciate all of you. I didn't think I was the best person to lead this effort, so whoever said just because you had a good idea doesn't mean you're meant to be a chair had a valid point. But I stepped up to be the chair, and I've been here all this time, and so have my line sisters. I think we needed help and advice from our big sisters, but, honestly, you prophtyes have not been here. If I recall, you guys haven't done that many projects, which is why you needed a new, innovative one in the first place. And we have been working hard. I'm sure there's something we're doing that you like, and you can comment on and figure out how we can blend the two ideas together to get a successful program. No one side is completely right, and no one side is completely wrong. We're Beta Gamma Pi, Alpha chapter. We are not divided, we're united. Can we act like it?"

Smiles shone throughout the room, and heads started

nodding. I didn't know where we were gonna go from here, but it looked like we were gonna work through our differences for the common good of the sorority. For that, I took a deep breath and was proud of myself for stepping up and being the chair. We all had worth. We all were needed. And it seemed we all were gonna work together.

I thought to myself, *Go, girl!*

Taking charge and exercising leadership in the right way was really working out. We weren't getting any new guys to participate, but we were going to add the swimsuit competition. I mean, even my line had to admit that the thought of the tasteful trunks on fine, chiseled black men was extremely appealing. And with sorors willing to work together, we can focus on making the event all we want it to be.

My line sisters were invited to the alumnae chapter's Collegiate Sorority Meeting Day. My mom had been on me, and she was hyped about their event like the spokesperson advertising for world peace and togetherness. "Hailey, please bring your friends. It's gonna be a great meeting. We just want to show you guys a little something to love and also expose you to what the alumni level is like. Dress in your finest business attire and be ready for us to love on you all."

I guess there was such a long time between when sorors finished their collegiate experience and when they joined the alumni chapter that they were trying to find a way to bridge the gap. Knowing how much this meant to my mom, my line sisters and I went. When we got there and saw the

tables full of gifts for the neophytes, we were all smiles—
we wouldn't have gotten a thing if we hadn't shown up.
Not that we had gone there to get something, but we were
pretty psyched to receive any type of paraphernalia.

However, all the excitement waned not even five minutes after the beautiful ceremony occurred. I thought Alpha
chapter had it going on with our properties, candles, and
pomp and circumstance. But this alumni chapter had the
silk purple and turquoise robes outlined in the glitz and
glamour to make you think you were in the presence of
royalty. No sooner had we renewed our vow and the
meeting officially begun than the President gave a report
that sent waves throughout the seats.

She said, "It's no secret that I, along with my officers,
have been in meetings over the summer with our Regional
and National Officers, letting them know we are not in
favor of another alumnae chapter coming to this area.
Giving up territory we've had for more than eighty years
is not an option. However, a group is here today who is
ready to lobby for the new chapter."

The room erupted with many disgruntled noises. A few
ladies stood and booed. These ladies were almost ready
to fight their own sorors who were trying to charter a
new chapter.

Finally the President hit the gavel and shouted, "Y'all
need to calm down. We gotta deal with this. You ladies
who live in this area, trying to start another chapter, need
recommendations from us to the Regional Coordinator.
And my recommendation is we're not willing to give up
that county."

My mother was sitting in front of me so I couldn't see

the expression on her face. We never talked about the strife alumnae chapters had. I didn't know why I thought it was a perfect world and their meetings had no issues. But there was so much grumbling going on, it made our rumblings at our meeting truly pale in comparison.

"Why do they want the chapter?" a soror stood up and said.

I hadn't been a member of Beta Gamma Pi long, but I knew that was out of order.

Another soror stood up behind her and said, "Well, I'm a part of the interest group's effort, and we want a chapter because those under y'all's service area haven't done any projects out there. While the area used to be predominantly white, things have changed over the last ten years. It needs a presence of its own, and Beta Gamma Pi needs to be out there full time, not partially or in nonexistence like it's been now."

Those two ladies were going head-to-head for a minute when finally the President hit the gavel. But it didn't do any good because the room got even more unruly. They were sisters, and they were acting like the two rival gangs from the club were trying to truly hurt one another.

Finally, I just stood to my feet to speak. Yeah, this wasn't my argument, this wasn't my battle to fight, but these were my sorors. This was crazy. I needed to end this!

"Excuse me! Can I say something, please?" I said, waving my hand in the air to try to get the Chapter President's attention.

Teddi was tugging on my suit. I shoved her hand off me. I needed to speak to try to calm everyone.

"Ladies, could y'all settle down and show respect? Let

the collegiate speak," said an alumni lady who sat on the other side of me.

"I don't know a lot about what is going on right now, being that I'm a new Beta Gamma Pi member. But I remember about twelve years ago when my mom was a charter member of this chapter. I was serving the ladies tea and drinks, and I would hear parts of the conversation taking place. If I recall, there was another chapter that had this service area, and they didn't want you guys to have it. And I think, looking back over all these years, even that chapter would admit they were wrong in wanting to prevent you ladies from going forward. Obviously— because look where you are today. So much service has been done. So I guess what I'm trying to say is while it's tough to give up territory or possibly lose future members, this chapter is growing—it's strong and thriving. Beta Gamma Pi should be about giving more and expanding. Don't you wanna make it easier for another chapter than this chapter had it?" Ladies were all listening and nodding, and I personally thought of my own challenges and continued. "Why can't the newcomer in Beta Gamma Pi ever get support? Gosh!"

## POMP

When I was done speaking, there was thunderous applause from all parts of the room. I didn't say what I'd said—from my heart—to get any accolades—as much as I wanted them to acknowledge what I said, take in what I said, and be ready to support growth. However, they kept clapping. At last they settled down, and there was a recommendation from a lady in their chapter not to fight the steering committee's wishes to have part of their territory charter a new chapter. It was seconded by my mother, and no one opposed the decision; it was unanimously voted upon to help the new effort.

After the meeting, a lady from the steering committee came over to me and said, "Oh, my gosh. You know, so many times women in chapters don't say anything because they wanna go along to get along, but sometimes we need to hear from the mouth of babes. You had a fresh, honest perspective we needed to hear. You understand the heart of what we're about. I'm glad you spoke, told the truth, shared your mind. You did it, soror! And because of it you blessed us to move forward."

My mom ran up to me and gave me a big hug and kiss. My line sisters gave me high fives but quickly moved over to the gift table. Pulling me away from my girls, my mom ushered me over to her Chapter President.

And the lady, who at first had been unmoved about not wanting to give up her territory and share, now had a change of heart and said, "Hi, I'm Soror Walker. Thank you."

"For what?" I said.

"For calling a spade a spade, keeping me honest about what Beta Gamma Pi should really be about in the first place. I had a lot of people over the last few years telling me, 'Don't lose territory on your watch.' I guess I bought into the hype and forgot about the principle that says why giving up territory is the best thing for the new chapter and for us. I don't know if you're planning on staying in the area. Your sister just joined our chapter earlier this year. So please consider us as your alumni home. If there is a new chapter, we don't wanna lose someone like you."

I just smiled and said, "Thanks. And thank you for allowing me to speak."

Teddi rushed over to us and said, "I'm sorry, but may I borrow her for a quick second?"

"Yes, sure. Now, you girls know you are welcome here anytime. We don't want you to just be here because we're giving out gifts," Soror Walker said, being the spunky President she was onstage.

"Yes, ma'am," Teddi said.

"Girl, what's up? You seem frustrated."

"We gotta hurry and get back to the chapter room."

"I don't know what you mean," I said to her, my eyes squinted.

"I don't know. Cassidy just called and said we need to get there, and quick."

In my gut, I felt it had something to do with the Mr. Beta contest. It took the five of us about twenty minutes to get to the chapter room. As soon as we walked through the door, Sam snatched me.

She said, "What the heck is going on, Hailey? I mean, are you monitoring what's going on in your committee?"

"Yeah," I said, thinking I had charged everyone with a task. I thought I'd had a good hold on everything. What could be the problem? I gave her a look like *Okay, what's up?*

Then she handed me a flier with our symbols on a guy's chest. "This is absolutely unacceptable! This guy is practically wearing nothing here! He is not a soror."

"I don't know who did that," I said to her, totally stunned.

"Yeah, we didn't do that," Quisa said, just as thrown off as I was.

All of a sudden, Connie entered the door, ranting. "Why did you summon me here?"

Sam said, "Somebody saw you putting up these posters,

Connie. You didn't get this approved. You can't put this up."

"I'm with promotions. People love the ad. Plus, the chair is cool with it," she said, pointing to me.

"Connie, I never saw it! Nor did the committee," I said, being clear she never showed me the sheet. "When did I approve this?"

"No, no, no," she said, getting defensive. "I told you I could get the people here, and you told me to go make it happen. So I got fliers, and I'm making it happen. Everybody's been stopping me asking me about the flier—that's why the word is out. This show is going to be hot. And don't trip on protocol. So what—I didn't show it to you all. I'm getting results. This ad is selling tickets," Connie said as she snatched the poster from Sam's hand.

Sam snatched it back. "Don't take anything out of my hand. This guy is not a member of Beta Gamma Pi, and he's sporting our symbols on his chest like he is."

Connie defended, "No, it says 'Sponsored by Beta Gamma Pi.' Don't you see 'sponsored by' over here on the right?"

"No, all I can see is the guy's chest. We're supposed to be about the business of BGP, not about 'come and sex me up.'" Sam turned to me. "I mean, what are you advertising here, Hailey? How come you didn't see this? Everything is supposed to come to me before it's put out there."

"Me, me, me, me, me," Connie taunted Sam. "It's *our* chapter, or has the power diluted your already power-hungry brain?"

"Whatever, Connie, don't show you're jealous. I'm the President, and I know you don't like it, but that's the way it is. And all these need to be removed now," Sam forcefully said as she moved closer to Connie's face.

"Then nobody will be in the audience, because these neophytes sure don't know how to make it happen," Connie said, stepping into Sam's space as well.

The two of them got closer to each other—everything I was trying to avoid. They were so big, trying to out-talk each other—so loud, so boisterous. It was just unsisterly. It wasn't about what the President was saying, it was how she was saying it. Connie had great intentions, but she was wrong with how she was trying to convey them. Because it couldn't go one hundred percent her way, she didn't want help at all. Maybe this was all a little too much for me.

Out of frustration, I said, "You know what? Forget this. I tried as chair, and I can't do this anymore. I quit."

"Whatever. Let her go!" Connie called out as I walked toward the door to exit our sorority room.

I hadn't said I was quitting to bluff. I wasn't thinking they'd come and beg me to stay. Nobody did that anyway. Obviously, I wasn't being an effective leader, and sometimes that was the problem, in my opinion, when it came to people leading anything. They never knew how to step aside and do what was best, not just for themselves, but for the group. Sometimes fresh blood made it easier to get the job done.

When I got outside, the rain hit my face. Though I wasn't having a pity party, I didn't feel happy. The majority of the time I insisted on an umbrella to keep dry. No, not this time. Now I needed the rain to cleanse me, free me from this stress and drama. The more wet I became, the fewer worries I was supposed to feel—but then things seemed worse.

"Hailey, wait up! I gotta get my umbrella up, girl!" Teddi called from somewhere behind me, but I wasn't stopping. I was going home to get in some studying before our midterms. "Okay, see, you're gonna catch the flu. You don't have on a coat, it's raining, and you're walking in the rain like it ain't wintertime. You live with me, girl, and I'm not getting sick. Get under this umbrella, Miss Stubborn."

"I just wanna be alone for a minute, Teddi, seriously."

"Listen," she said as she stopped me from walking. "When this school term started back in the fall, I really wanted to be SGA President. I thought I could give the students here what we were missing—integrity, character, someone they could believe in and trust who would never give up on them and never let them down. Problem was I didn't have a plan, and then this guy came along, and he did have one. Now he has proven to be in it for the long haul. So I'm admitting I wasn't the best candidate." I looked at her like *Where are you going with this?* "We joined a sorority to make a difference. And I guess I'm learning I can be a good leader if I learn how to be a good follower. And I wouldn't be a good follower if I just let you walk off the job. This is your vision. You are supposed to see it through. So there have been a few bumps along this road—we need them to make us stronger. We need you."

"Whatever. You heard them back there. If they need this, they certainly don't need me. Oh, no, I'm through," I said, hoping Teddi would get the point.

"Come on, I'm kidnapping you."

"Where are we going?"

"For a little drive."

Disgusted with the thought of getting more soaked, I walked back with Teddi to her car. Whether I admitted it or not, I really wanted to see where she was taking me. I guess after asking her numerous times Teddi began to ignore my question. Playing it smart, I just sat back, let Teddi drive, and prayed inwardly I could get myself together. Feeling like a failure had me really down.

Riding toward the projects, I had no clue where we were going. We were at a trailer park that needed to be condemned. The place looked unlivable. Yet kids were playing in the yard, so I knew someone lived there.

"You put me in charge of finances," she said, "and so I came out to see this family because I wanted to present to the sorority what we could do with the money we raised and how we could best help them."

"Where are we?"

"We're at Ms. King's place."

"I thought she stayed somewhere else," I said, remembering the decent place I had visited her at during the Thanksgiving holiday.

"She got kicked out of that place, and now she lives here."

"But half the windows are boarded up."

"Exactly, but they're in there. Girl, it's so sad."

When we went inside, Ms. King was happy to see Teddi.

It felt good she remembered me when we'd had only the one visit. Teddi said she forgot something and headed back to the car.

Ms. King said, "So, girl, I don't just remember your pretty face. I also remember you were a little down. You better?"

I so wanted to crawl into her arms and yell, "No!" However, I knew looking at her tough situation that she didn't need to be weighed down with anyone else's bad news. So I assured her I was better.

"Good," she said as she extended her arms. "Come on, let Ms. King give you some love. Everybody needs a hug now and then to keep 'em feeling special."

When Teddi came back in, she had the kids trailing behind her. They were yelling for joy. Teddi had given each of them stuffed animals. I thought that was so sweet.

Teddi mumbled under her breath, "Don't tell anybody I'm doing this. How hilarious! Teddi giving out teddy bears. You better not say anything, Hailey!"

"But it's so nice, girl."

Ms. King's eyed watered, and she sank to her couch that had half a cushion. "Oh, Teddi, girl, this is so nice. Now them kids will stop asking for stuff for a bit. I'm just so glad y'all stopped by to help me. Don't nobody care. They always say there's a whole bunch of paperwork to file, and I can qualify for this and get approved for that. I don't know how to do that stuff! All I know is I got these children, and if it ain't one thing they need, it's another. I got more bills than I got money. I already lost one house and a daughter, and if I don't get it together, DFCS will come and take these kids from me. I don't know if they can survive losing me on top of losing they mama. Shoot, I don't know if I can survive it either."

By the time she finished speaking, water was all over my face, and it wasn't from the rain I had just come out of. We stayed there another hour. Teddi and I helped the two older children with their reading and math, and then we helped Ms. King clean up a little bit and assured her we could get her funds that could fix her holed floors and her broken window. We also knew she needed a refriger- ator and, if we could swing it, a washer and drier. I couldn't imagine going to the wash house, as she called it. Before we left, we took pictures. Teddi and I knew the chapter needed to see the devastation.

As soon as we got in the car, Teddi just looked at me. She didn't have to say anything. She didn't have to make a big speech about me staying to make a difference. I just nodded and I knew, no matter how tough or uncomfort- able it may feel, that what we were doing was much big- ger than me. But what we were doing needed me to help get it done, and just like that I was back on board ready to chair the committee again.

Later that night, my line sisters showed up to the dorm Teddi and I shared.

"So, tell us you're not quitting," Evan said, obviously hoping the rumor wasn't true.

"I know we're all a hot mess to lead," Quisa said as she took my hand, "but we need you."

"And we're not letting you quit," Millie said, unusually strong. "So now what?"

"No use, you guys. She said she's never gonna participate as a collegiate Beta again," Teddi said, making me pick the pillow off the bed and toss it at her.

But it was cute to hear the other three moaning, groaning, and pleading for what they'd heard not to be the case. I tried to speak, but Teddi kept blocking me. Their faces did look truly sad. Finally, I shoved my silly friend out of the way.

"She's pulling y'all's leg. I did need to think, but Teddi made me see that together we can do this. Together we can do anything. I'm in. Check out these pictures, and you'll see why," I told them, pointing to the photos of the place Ms. King and the kids now called home.

We were all in tears as we took them through the pictures. The thought of any human living in an inhuman space sickened me. For about twenty minutes we just sat there hating all that Ms. King's family was going through. I actually thought we'd never smile again.

Then Evan lightened the mood when she said, "Well, let's go out and party."

"Party? Girl, you hear that storm outside? It's raining bad," I said, remembering I'd already been wet enough for one day.

"So what? We're alive. We're Betas. We just got our letters. The stitching is still tight on our jackets. We need to get out and let them see the latest line of Alpha chapter. Hailey, when we crossed we didn't go out as a line. Let's do it now," Evan said.

Teddi said, "I know you wanna go anyway. SGA is throwing a canned-food-drive party. You don't have to bring money, just food to help out the families who have been displaced by the tornado."

Quisa said, "I can't believe the food bank was destroyed."

"Yep, they're operating out of some warehouse, and food is extremely low," Teddi said, knowing more than me about the community I was supposed to be really in tune with.

I should've known something was up when the three of them came in looking cute for some reason. Though I knew I still had issues to deal with concerning the Chapter President and the prophytes, I couldn't hide out. And they would probably be at the party representing. Plus, the idea of seeing Covin . . . well, it excited me, too.

When the five of us got through the door fashionably late, the place was packed! The party was in the gym, and from freshmen to graduate students, there was barely room to move around. But there was a makeshift stage, and my uncle was standing up there with Covin.

President Webb said, "I've been the President of this school for five years. I've seen a lot of SGAs do great things. I've even seen some disappointments. But this year you guys are rallied behind this guy right here," he said as he raised Covin's hand. "And Mr. Randall is making a difference. Tomorrow the mayor of the city and a fire marshal will pick up the cans we collect tonight and take them to the remote food bank. Our donations will be distributed to needy families everywhere. I am all for college students completely enjoying their collegiate experience, and getting an education is first and foremost here. But tonight you deserve to have a good time. Not only has our graduation rate gone up the last two years, but what we've done to change the community will have an impact that will bless many. And for that you should be proud."

When my uncle finished his speech, everyone shouted and chanted Covin's name. He was looking so good! Jeans fitting him in all the right places. A button-down shirt that was neatly pressed yet open enough at the top to be sexy as I don't know what. I was missing him so much. We were in public, and I had to keep my feelings intact. I could only wish I was back in his place—this time with a different outcome.

Then my uncle called our homecoming queen to join Covin onstage. Covin took her hand and said, "This whole idea about the canned-food drive to help out the food bank—I couldn't have done it without this lady." He reached over to hug her and give her a kiss on the cheek.

I didn't notice my eyes watering up, but Teddi sure did. "You wanna be with the guy. You can't let someone else take your man, because if you're seeing what I'm seeing, she's all into him."

I tried so hard not to want him, but seeing him there with somebody else, what had I done? I did want him to be mine, but I had ended it. He was a guy going somewhere, and I could never hold him back, but I could also never hold back my extreme sadness.

Just as he began holding hands with our beautiful homecoming queen, I tried to get by without him seeing me.

This was his moment, and I didn't need to ruin it, but I couldn't take him being with another and getting all the accolades without me being by his side to share it with him. The crowd was all on his jock, and I had to get away from all that pomp.

## BE

I just couldn't be around him, but I wanted him so badly and was drawn to him more when I saw him in the arms of another. I had to get away from this awful scene and quickly erase it from my memory.

Teddi held my arm and said, "Where are you going? It's storming out there." I just shook my head in confusion and dashed away from the unbearable sight.

As soon as I was alone in the dark night, I looked to the sky and said, "Lord, I've been trying to go about my business and not think about Covin. Just as I feel I'm strong enough, You have me witness him being happy with someone else. You have to make her a gorgeous homecoming queen at that! That was a huge slap to my face. Why, when I had a good guy, could I not be smart? Why did I waste a good thing on an idiot? Help me, Lord, move past this and not trip."

Searching unsuccessfully in the crowded parking lot for my car, I suddenly remembered I hadn't driven. I turned back around to go inside to tell Teddi to take me home. Unfortunately, the steps to my path were cut short when I bumped into Covin himself.

"Why are you out here in the rain, Hailey? You're gonna catch pneumonia or something," he said, getting wet, too.

"You didn't have to come out here to check on me. I can clearly see you're with someone else now," I said, salty as chips.

"Are you crying?" he asked me as he lifted my chin. I just pulled away. "What's going on with you, Hailey? I know you're not upset that I'm with another girl."

"I know, I know, I know," I said, completely losing it. "I was the one who wanted to date other people."

"And from what I heard, you are already doing that."

I turned away, thinking, *And it didn't go as well as I planned*. He studied my face, and knew I'd made a terrible mistake. But he stood there with deep concern and didn't rub anything in my face.

But how could I have ever wanted another? I didn't know what to do next. I couldn't look back at him. I couldn't face him. The care he was showing, I didn't deserve. When we'd started months back, we'd barely had time to mess up our good thing. However, I'd just treated us like a used piece of paper on the floor—picked it up and thrown it in the trash. But now I wanted it to be fresh and new again. I just wasn't sure if it was right or fair of me to ask him.

"What is it you want?" he asked as he came closer and

wrapped me in his arms. "Tell me what you want from me, Hailey."

"It doesn't matter what I want. I messed up, okay? You were a great guy, and I guess because I hadn't had a boyfriend in a long time, I didn't know how to treat one when I had a gift."

"Well," he said as he held me tighter and tried to stop me from shivering, "I haven't stopped thinking about you."

Then someone yelled out his name from the gymnasium door. "Covin! Covin, are you out here?"

We ran like two elementary school kids trying to hide from their principal after school. Being silly and giddy, I fell into his lap. I wasn't bothered by the cold, wet rain, because the connection we had warmed me all over.

"You need to go tell her something," I whispered to him.

Being coy and mannish, he said, "There's so much going on inside, she'll turn around and look for me in there."

"So, are y'all dating or something?"

"What, are you jealous now?" he said, wiping my brow.

"I mean, I can't pull you away from somebody else."

"It's been only a couple months since we haven't been together, and all I wanted to do was this," he said as he placed his hands on both sides of my face, pulled my face to his, and allowed our lips to lock.

I usually wasn't a fan of the rain, but out there, with him, I let the water hit my face, and it relaxed me. Amidst all that water, it was like it had brought Covin and me back together by washing away all the strife. I had gotten a second chance, and I wasn't gonna mess it up this time.

"I wanna be with you," I said to him as he stroked my face.

"But we're both soaked. I need to get back in here to this party. Afterward we can hook up."

I took his hands and put them around my waist and then took to kissing him. After a long encounter I said, "No, not later. Now. I want to be with you."

He patted his coat jacket, pulled out some keys, and smiled wider than the Grand Canyon. "Are you sure?" he said to me as he licked his lips at me.

I was still pure, and I'd be lying if I said I wasn't a little nervous. But being in his arms, a place I didn't think I'd ever be again, was like heaven. Feeling the passion that extended from one part of my body to the other, I knew more than anything that I was ready—so much so that I was ready to give it up on the concrete ground.

But when I went to unbutton his pants, he said, "You deserve way better than this. And, for real, we would be really sick in this nasty weather. Don't you think you need to take your car home?"

"I didn't drive," I said to him.

"Well, you need to let someone know where you're going."

"I'll text my girls later."

He kissed me again, and we headed off in his car.

Forty-five minutes later we were in a hotel suite in the center of downtown Little Rock. He had gotten us a room on the top floor of a hotel. Opening the doors to our lavish suite with the room card key, I was engulfed in a cloud of bliss. The room screamed of freshness, and the spacious bedding area released aromatherapy. Sheets and the comforter of every shade of white was piled high atop of the king-size bed. The view of the pretty city made me feel like a queen. I was so impressed.

Before my sophomore year, merely being with a guy in a hotel room ready to give it up would have been out of my character. Never, ever had I done something so impulsive. Going out with Morgan before knowing him fully was stupid, but this felt safe, beautiful, and right. We hadn't even done anything.

As Covin called room service, I went over to the balcony and prayed. *Lord, I want this night to be as special as You would allow it. Please be with me as I share my all.*

"What are you thinking?" he asked me as he kissed my neck.

"I'm thinking I wanna give you every part of me. You've given me your heart. You've given me a second chance, and now it's time I became the gracious one. As a kid I thought about the moment I'd lose my virginity. But never did I imagine being in a hotel suite, treated like a queen."

The doorbell rang, and he told me to go ahead and take a shower. When the hot water hit my body, I really got excited. But then when the doorknob turned, and he asked if he could join me, every part of me felt alive. I didn't say yes, but because I didn't say no, moments later every inch of Covin's body was mine to view. And, boy, did I like what I saw! Why I'd ever thought Morgan was sexier was crazy, too.

"You're even more beautiful than I'd imagined," he said as he checked me out.

I wasn't nervous at his gaze. My heart just started racing as his hand touched every part of me. He turned off the water, scooped me out of the tub, threw a robe around me, and led me to the bed. He eased himself on top of my body that desired him so and looked into my eyes that spoke of my love.

"You don't have to do this, you know."

I kissed him, and he kissed me back. The night was warm, passionate, sexy, steamy, inviting, exuberant, and ours. The slight discomfort was felt for seconds. And the second time around was even better than the first. I knew when he called my name I was in love. Again it was confirmed that this was right. This was wonderful. This had become a night I would never forget.

Two days later, when I woke up back in my own bed, I still felt like I was in heaven. I replayed my magical weekend over and over; I regretted none of it. But I did wonder why Covin had dropped me off at six in the evening, said he'd call, and it was now eighteen hours later and there was no phone call.

"Okay, so you wanna tell me where you've been all weekend?" Teddi said to me as she grilled me when she saw my eyes open. "You go to a party with us, leave all frustrated, have us tell the big sisters you're gonna chair the contest after all, text me an hour later telling me you're okay, and then you're dead asleep when I come home, thinking I'm not gonna wake you?"

I wanted to say, "Girl, you're not my mom—I'm a grown woman now. I had an experience that was private and special, and I wanna keep it that way." However, I knew she loved me and probably had been sick with worry.

So to get her off my back, I smiled and said, "I was with Covin. We worked everything out. You said I was out cold last night—did he happen to call me?"

Teddi looked up at the ceiling like she was trying to think back, but I knew he had called. He had to. I was so knocked out I probably didn't hear the phone ring. Because sleep had been the last thing I had gotten while I was with him, Teddi had known I was too tired and didn't want to wake me. That had to be it.

I was too dumbfounded when she said, "No, Hailey. Nobody called."

I looked over at the phone that was on the nightstand between both of our twin beds and said, "Well, was it off the hook or something?"

*There had to be an explanation why I didn't receive his call,* I thought to myself. Then it dawned on me like a ray of sunshine sparks a new day, that he had used another method. I hit my hand to my forehead like I should have had a V8 and ran over to my cell phone. Surely, that was it. He'd called me, and it had been on vibrate or silent.

After I disappointedly checked my voice mail and text messages to find out Covin hadn't contacted me, Teddi put her two cents in the situation. "Why are you even stressing like you're married to him or something? So what—he didn't call. Why are you freaking out? He's still got a reason to chase you, right?"

"I'm not freaking out," I said, clearly freaking out as I held an upset look on my face.

It took me a while to look at Teddi. When we locked

eyes, I might as well have told her I'd given away the milk for free. I hoped I wasn't a fool.

Indirectly telling me to move on and not stress it, Teddi said, "Come on. Some of us are heading to the library to study. Get dressed."

I wanted to tell her to go on without me so I could call Covin and see if he was okay, but I could sense I was being a little paranoid. Maybe he was just as tired as I was.

So I went on to study and had a great time with my line sisters as we planned more for the upcoming contest, and they filled me in on all the dirt in the chapter. It seemed Connie and Sam had had another incident and gone at each other. As they talked about it, I really tuned them out as I looked at my phone, wanting it to ring badly.

The next few days came and went. And in terms of communication with Covin, it was more of the same—no phone call. Finally, I reached out to him. And when I dialed him the first time, I got his voice mail. I was addicted because on the hour, for seven hours, I kept trying him. I couldn't figure out why the brother wasn't calling me back.

Cassidy came over to our place later that night so Teddi and I could fill her in on the particulars surrounding the contest. "You seem pretty occupied," she said as she apparently tried to get my attention several times and I was out of it.

"Been like that for the last couple days," Teddi added. "She must have her head too far up Covin's—"

"Okay, okay!" I said as Cassidy laughed. "This isn't a joke."

"Sorry, girl. Just trying to liven you up," Teddi said.

"What's up? Talk to me," Cassidy said.

I said, "There's nothing to talk about."

"Obviously, there's something to talk about. You're visibly shaken. Come on, let's step out into the hall and walk off some of this."

I guess it was bothering me more than I knew because when we stepped outside I just blurted, "I don't understand! I gave him everything, and he hasn't called!"

"Having sex with a guy is a big step. It's not something that should be taken lightly. The whole school knows what happened to me last year."

"The AIDS scare?" I said.

"Yeah," she said. "I wish I could take back the night I spent with that jerk, but I can't. And what you described to me seems like it was a great time. Did you guys use . . ."

"Yeah, we were straight with that. I'm not saying we used the word *love*, but I didn't think he was trying to hit it and quit it, you know?"

"Well, don't pressure it. Don't run him away. You left him a few messages, so give him time to respond. If it's right and it's what you feel it is, it'll be."

## GARGANTUAN

It had been five days since I'd heard from Covin. I was walking on campus from my last class, passing by the SGA office. I was stopped in my tracks when I saw his car parked outside, but I kept replaying in my head what Cassidy had said. "Don't pressure it. Give him time to respond." But it had been five days! I thought we had something special, and he at least owed me an explanation as to why I'd been dissed.

Instead of going about my business, I walked inside. There was a purse on the desk where the SGA secretary, Barbie, was supposed to sit, but she was nowhere in sight. Then I thought back to a few months ago when she was really into helping Covin set up. Sure enough, I saw from way down the hall that Barbie was gazing in his eyes, eating up every word he put out. Whether he was for it or not, she wanted him. As I approached the SGA office doors, I heard voices.

"You are doing the best job ever," Barbie said as her playfulness brought out a laugh in Covin.

I didn't want to make the old door creak, but I had to open it. He had to see me. I had to know what was really going on. To me, they were getting just a little too chummy. Was she the reason he hadn't given me a call? As soon as I touched the knob, they looked my way.

"Can't you knock?" Barbie said, very aggravated.

"Hey, lady," Covin said as he walked over to the door, completely ignoring the fact that she was irritated that I was there.

"Hey," I said halfheartedly.

I wanted him to understand that he had a lot of explaining to do, but I didn't want her to know we had problems. He opened the door all the way and gestured for me to come inside. Barbie looked so salty, irritated, almost upset that I had interrupted their time again. But, whatever—like I cared.

"Can you excuse us?" I said to her when she would not leave.

She looked at Covin.

"Yeah. I need to talk to my girl," he said as he leaned over and gave me a kiss on the cheek.

As soon as she left the room, I closed the door behind her. It actually sounded like I slammed it. Disappointed and shocked at my attitude, Covin looked at me like *What's up with all that?*

"You know what, let's just cut to the chase. Obviously, you're busy. You and your secretary working in here late after hours while everyone else is gone. Did you not get my messages? Did you not get my calls? Why didn't you call me back?"

"Okay, hold up. Hailey, I got your calls. I was gonna get back to you, but can't you see I'm, like, in the middle of stuff here?" he pitifully tried to explain.

"No, I just see the two of you shooting the breeze. Where's the work?"

"Well, we're catching up because I've been with my dad in session at the state capitol. I got to shadow him some."

"It would've been great if you told me where you were gonna be these past few days."

"I've been thinking about you," he said as he reached out to touch my face.

Stepping away from his hand, I said, "I sure can tell that."

"Come on, Hailey. Don't make a big deal out of it."

At that moment, I had to hold back the tears. He had told me not to make a big deal of it. Was he crazy? Was he tripping? I mean, seriously, I had given him my body, my mind, my soul. Now, after he'd gotten it, it was like he'd thrown me away. I felt like trash or something. He couldn't even return my calls letting me know where he'd been. It was like he'd moved on to the next big thing. Screw whatever I thought.

"I can see you're upset, and that's not my intent. I'm sorry I hurt your feelings, but I gotta admit all the calls and you coming in here without calling is a little much. It's a little too overwhelming. I don't wanna lose my strong Hailey, the one who couldn't serve with me as my director of community relations because her plate runneth over. You know what I'm saying?"

I'm glad a tear didn't fall. I didn't wanna give him the satisfaction of seeing me cry. He was saying he liked me when I wasn't all over him. The problem was I couldn't get the fact that he'd been all over me out of my mind. Could I go back to the Hailey that gave him distance?

"Take care of whatever you gotta take care of," I said as I left.

We had a big issue between us. Covin called for me, but I kept past a nosy Barbie and kept walking. I didn't know how it could be fixed or if it could be fixed at all.

"So, what do I owe to this surprise?" my uncle, President Webb, said to me as I made my way over to his office after seeing Covin.

I tried to be tough and say, "I just wanted to see you."

But I couldn't hold back the tears. I turned away, hoping he wouldn't see me. He came to me and said, "Okay, something's wrong. I'm excited you came to see your uncle. We may not have spent as much time together as we did your freshman year, but I know when something's wrong with my girl. Let me take you to dinner so we can talk."

I nodded, knowing he was just the medicine I needed. I remembered how close we were last year. We had formed a tight bond when I was little. I could always talk to him, especially since my dad was in the Navy and wasn't there a lot. My uncle would come and get me and make me feel like I was the most special girl on Earth. I guess, for a second, now that I was all grown up, I needed him to make me feel like that again, particularly since Covin had made me feel like something cheap.

My uncle asked so many questions on the way to the restaurant. When I didn't answer them, he just started talking about himself. "So, my divorce is final now."

"There are so many marriages ending in divorce, I wonder why people even bother," I finally opened up and said. "Your wife was such a jerk, only caring about herself."

"Wait, now. I have to take some of the responsibility for our downfall. More people need to quit looking on the other side of things and instead look in the mirror. When I got married to your aunt, I wined and dined her. She was my world. Then I got this job, my dream job, and a part of me forgot the fact that I had to take care of my dream woman. I didn't balance them well. And while I can't say she was completely without fault either, I can say, had I been on my job and done a better balancing act, I wouldn't be alone," he confessed, being more transparent than clear tape on a present.

I caught a lump in my throat. Feeling for my uncle was hard enough. He was now hurting that his marriage was over. He'd always been so strong for me; seeing him down wasn't easy. To make me feel even worse, he pulled into the same place I was held up in a couple months back when the gangs were trying to kill each other and when the tornado blew through.

"Look, it's a grand reopening. This is great, right? Our state is getting back on its feet. What once was a club is now a restaurant. The paper said the owner made the change to reach for a more professional clientele."

"This is good to see them open. I'm all for economic development. It's just . . ."

"Oh, my gosh, Hailey. You were here during the shootout. We can go to another place," he said, shaking his head. I could tell he felt bad he didn't remember.

"No, it's cool," I said, realizing that I had to learn to face difficult situations. "I want to go in and see if the manager's here. It is huge to see that it's open again."

As soon as we went in, we were greeted by the manager. He remembered me instantly and offered to comp my meal. Trying to support, my uncle wouldn't hear of it.

"Your niece is a brave young lady. The life of my bartender was spared because she risked her life to make sure we helped him. The guy was not only my employee but my friend as well. For your caring and help, I am forever grateful. She's got a big heart. You have to let me give you my best table and an appetizer and dessert," the manager pleaded.

"If you must," my uncle said. "We're just happy to see your business up and running again."

Soon after the manager left our table, a waiter followed to take our drink order. I asked for water with lemon, and my uncle asked for sweet tea. The minute I thought the questioning was over, my adamant uncle pulled a fast one.

"So what's up?" he said with a look that said *I'm not going to leave this alone.*

"I guess I just don't understand men. And I do wanna spare you the details," I said, realizing I did need to keep some of this private.

"Well, the same stuff your dad and I have been preaching for years about men is still true. And I hope you're not out there giving it up to them."

"Unc!"

"Don't uncle me. Men still like the chase, and they respect the ones that make them work for it."

I just turned away, and when I looked up there was someone coming over to us with two large shakes. "We didn't order those," I said.

"No, the manager told me who you are," the man said. "You might not remember me, but I'm the bartender whose life you saved that night. I just wanna thank you and tell you you changed my life. I now know it's not just about me, it's about making this world a better place. For the longest time, I asked myself why I had that big scare, and I had to admit that I had been selfish. My mom had used her savings to put me through school, and I'd partied and flunked out. Thanks to you, I'm saving up my money so I can go back to college next year."

"That sounds wonderful, son," my uncle said. "I'm president of Western Smith College, and that is great news."

"Yes, sir. I'm planning to make you proud. Enjoy your shakes on me; I don't wanna take up any more of your time."

"I don't like hearing you risked your life to save somebody," my uncle said, "but I'm really proud of you, Hailey. This thing with your guy—I don't know much about where y'all are, but don't lose who you are. Guys are great, but don't be all up under him, and don't run him off. When you are the Hailey Grant I know and who that bartender was so thankful for, any young man going somewhere can clearly see he'd be better off with you as his girl. But sometimes women become so boy crazy, they lose themselves, and they can't see that's not attractive. You're smarter than that, and I know that won't happen to you. And if it has, reprioritize, and you'll get the guy you want. Take it from a man who has played the field and gotten back in the game. No matter how old, young, crazy, or in love a man is, he wants a woman who gives him his space and allows him to appreciate their time apart so he can long for her and treat her better once they get back together."

I got up and hugged him tight. My uncle had given me some crucial advice. Now I could understand the medicine that Covin was trying to give me to cure our weakened relationship. It wasn't about me learning how to play the game, it was about me understanding that there was more to life than him—there was me. And I needed to get back to loving myself.

"You mean you got time to go with us to a sorority event?" Teddi sarcastically said to me as I hopped in the car with my line sisters to go to the statewide Founders' Day Celebration after days of exile.

"Lay off her," Quisa said. "She's in the car already."

I had been sulking for the last week. I wasn't going to defend myself, because I needed to be scolded. "She's straight," I said to Quisa. "I deserve it. You get what you give. I haven't been giving a lot to you guys, so I just have to take it and deal with it."

"Well, I don't wanna hear it," Quisa responded and turned the music up. "None of us are perfect."

When we got to the luncheon at the exquisite hotel downtown, we all were given blue candles representing

the blue sapphire in our beloved sorority pin that sym-
bolized our commitment to unending service. As we entered the ballroom, with theater-style seats and decorated
in Beta Gamma Pi paraphernalia, I took in its lovely
view. Every year during a five-year rotation, a different
founder was honored, and that year we focused on that
founder's major passion. This year was the last in the five-
year cycle, and we were dwelling on public service, the
one thing that had drawn me into Beta Gamma Pi.

As I listened to our State Director go on and on about
giving, a part of my heart boiled over. I had given a lot
since I had become a Beta. I'd tried to let others lead, I'd
risked my life a few times to help others, and I still wasn't
completely happy. It just seemed like when you gave so
much, and for the right reasons, life should be great, life
should be grand, and life should render nothing but hap-
piness. If I had to live all the drama, yet I was a good person, a part of me wondered what the heck was the point?

And just at that moment, the State Director said, "As
the flame of public service gets passed throughout the
room, let us each recommit ourselves to why we give so
freely—just like our founder Louise Lindsey spent her life
tutoring underprivileged kids to give them a better chance
and giving them piano lessons so they could understand
how the arts could help instill greatness in them. I remember Ms. Lindsey saying, 'Give from the heart and what
you'll receive will be immeasurable.'"

At that moment, the flame from Teddi's green candle
was pointed to my empty wick. "Thank you for pushing
me," I said to her as our candles united.

She leaned over to hug me and give me a kiss. "Hailey,

you got it going on, girl. You're beautiful, you're smart, and, more than anything, you care."

The State Director continued. "Ladies, I got it. I finally got it. Soror Lindsey taught us that public service doesn't help just the person in need, but it helps the person who's giving because you're stronger and see and understand the miracle of knowing you can't make it in this life alone. We're not here to stay. But while we are here, give more than your share, and give more than you take, and you can have true peace."

Wow. Now I finally got it. This life wasn't about me. I enjoyed more when I had an open heart. To feel, care, and love—to truly understand that—was big. Huge. Gargantuan.

## PLAN

"Okay, so what is the emergency, and why are all these cars here?" I asked myself as I pulled up into my mom's driveway.

My mom had called me an hour before and asked me to come over. Though she would not explain the emergency, she did have urgency in her voice. I'd immediately gotten dressed, dropped what I was about to do, and headed her way.

Driving to her place, so many things were running through my mind. Was my dad okay? Were Hayden and her fiancé having issues? Or did my uncle open his mouth and tell my mom she needed to talk to me? However, all those things were personal, and seeing tons of cars in the yard with Beta Gamma Pi tags on the backs of the vehicles knocked out all those things I was thinking. So what was up? Like a kindergartner gets apprehensive about going to school on the first day, I felt just as weird about going inside.

As soon as I stepped out of the car, my phone rang. To my surprise, it was Covin. He had been calling me over the past few days, and I hadn't returned his calls or listened to his messages. It wasn't about me being rebellious or teaching him a lesson, it was just me taking time out for me and not being so pushy anymore, even when he initiated our time.

But I didn't need to fool myself. I did miss him, so I picked up the phone and said, "Hello?"

"Hey, girl. What's up? You put me down," Covin said in a joking way, yet at the same time I knew he was serious.

"Can I just be honest with you?" I said, looking to the sky for strength.

"Yeah, sure."

"I just thought a lot about what you said, and I owe you an apology for being your stalker."

He laughed. "Yeah, but I didn't want you to go MIA on a brother."

"I promise you I won't. Just been busy lately," I said.

He said, "So, can I see you? I do need some affection."

*No, he didn't have the nerve to go there,* I thought to myself. "Okay, you're quiet. You're the one who said we should be honest. I miss you."

"Well, I'm at my mom's right now, so it can't be tonight."

"Okay. What about tomorrow?"

"Tomorrow I got sorority stuff. Sorry."

"How about this? Please say Saturday night you'll go with me to my parents' house."

Now he was freaking me out. He had really surprised me. He had gone from basically wanting a booty call to asking for a first-class date to meet his folks. Was I awake and not dreaming?

"What? Really? Okay, yeah, I'll go," I said. "I'll call you later so I can get the details."

"Okay, cool. And, Hailey?"

"Yeah?"

"I really do miss you."

"Okay," I said and hung up.

I actually felt pretty good as I walked through my mom's front door. My chest was poked out, and I was proud of myself. Though I missed him, too, I didn't need to let him know it. Again, I hated we had to play games, but now I realized I couldn't show him all the cards in my hand when I was dealt another round. I was gonna play smarter. And it looked like I was winning.

As soon as I got inside, my mom said, "There you are, girl. The meeting's almost over. It took you forever to get here."

"Oh, give the girl a break," one lady said.

"Hi, everyone!" I said as I waved, still not understanding what any of this was about.

My mom said, "Hailey, you remember our Chapter President?"

"Yes. Hello, Soror Walker. You look lovely today," I said, admiring her St. John purple pants suit.

"Well, thanks," Soror Walker said. "We just wanna tell you we think you are a dynamic young lady."

I was very skeptical, but I nodded in appreciation. I'd done so much growing up over the last six months. However, I felt far from dynamic.

"And I don't know if you know yet, but no one has put their name in the hat to run for the Second National Vice President office at our upcoming convention," Soror Walker said, smiling at me as though she wanted me to like her plan.

As I squinted my eyes, I first wondered what any of that had to do with me, but I wasn't a dummy. The way they were all sort of salivating at the mouth was like they wanted to put me up for that office. I wasn't too sure about this.

So before they could go any further, I said, "My sister tried out for that when I was in high school, and it crushed her when she didn't win. I'm sure there'll be lots of folks who run on the floor, but I'm not going to be one of them. Thanks though."

When I turned around to walk out, my mom stopped me dead in my tracks. "Hailey Grant, get back in here! These ladies came to talk to you, and you're going to listen."

"We can never guarantee a victory," Soror Walker said in her more presidential voice. "Let me remind you, your sister went at the election with just her collegiate chapter. We want to arm you with ammunition. We wanna get behind you as the alumnae chapter and use all our connections throughout the United States. Some folks owe our chapter some favors. Besides, you helped open our eyes to what this sorority is supposed to be about. Just think about it. But we do need to know by the end of next week so we can get a campaign going and be ready, come May."

I thanked them appropriately, fellowshipped with them a little over my mom's tea and crumpets, and took it all in as I headed back to my campus. I was in awe, wondering if I was even gonna try. Could their plan work, and was I worthy?

*Lord,* I prayed, *give me direction and help me figure this one out.*

I really had no idea what to do and needed some kind of guidance to get me through this tough decision. He was the only One who could show me the way. I needed it to be shown soon so I'd know where I was headed.


"Okay, okay, guys, let's not panic. So what—we're not completely on target for this project. That doesn't mean all is lost. We gotta think positive," I said to my line sisters as we tried to assess where we were with the committee plans.

Teddi said, "Well, I'm in charge of the finances, and the whole contest is about making it a fund-raiser for our chapter so we could really help Ms. Mayzee's family. I'm just hoping we break even. That means the little one thousand dollars the chapter gave us to print the invitations, to do the marketing, to buy the decorations for the stage, and so forth would work out well if we could recoup that. No contestant is saying they're able to raise a lot of money."

"Well, Beta Gamma Pi Week is also coming up in a couple months, and the majority of the chapter is working on that. Connie and the rest of the prophytes that said they wanted to help us with this and that when it came down to it haven't even been to another meeting," I informed my sisters.

"See, Hailey?" Teddi stepped in and said. "The only thing I'm saying is that you need to put a hold on the pro-phytes helping us—even you trying to please the Chapter President, asking her what she thinks of this and that."

"Well, I mean, she *is* the Chapter President, Teddi."

Teddi continued. "I know, and it's great that you want everybody's opinion, but there's only us five working this thing. I sorta feel like they want us to fail."

"Maybe we should call the whole thing off," Quisa uttered with a deflated look worse than a balloon with no air.

"No, guys, we're not going to cancel this. If it's just the five of us, we can figure this out. We may not raise as much money as we projected, but we're not gonna lose money for this chapter either. This idea will work, and you guys know with ticket sales that people splurge at the last minute. Let's not panic about the price."

The four of them kept talking amongst each other, as though all hope was lost. Though I was trying to keep them encouraged, they kept saying one negative thing after another. Yes, we were now in it alone, and maybe they were right. Maybe some people did wanna see us fail. But we were in charge of this contest. We had not abandoned it like our other sisters, and if we pulled together and started working together as hard as we could, we were going to have some great results.

So I got out a sheet of paper and wrote down the eight candidates' names we had left. Teddi called out where they were with money, and it looked bleak. Some boys had reported they had sold only one, and a couple said they hadn't collected a dime.

"We've got to help these guys raise some money. Even if we don't get them to the minimum we wanted, we need to have everyone bring in something respectable," I said.

"No, we can't do this. College kids don't have two nickels to rub together to make a dime right now! We need backup," Teddi said. "I've been working with them, and my cup runneth out of ideas."

And then it dawned on me: I had just been in a room with all the alumni ladies who were telling me to rely on them if I ever needed something, and right now I needed something bad. They were the queens of throwing a benefit barbecue, a collection car wash, or a bake sale to help raise money. I quickly went through my BlackBerry to find the President's number.

"Hello, Hailey Grant," Soror Walker said without me saying hi myself. "You're calling to tell me you're taking us up on our offer."

"I'm calling to take you up on your offer, but not the one you're thinking about," I responded shyly.

"Okay, well, explain."

"I'm heading the Mr. Beta Gamma Pi contest and we're raising money to support a struggling family in need, and the contestants need money to stay in school, but the problem is all our gents are having trouble getting their money up. I was just wondering if . . ."

"You want our help? Oh, my gosh, we love those kinds of things, and we're not doing our annual Pearl contest this year. You were a Pearl a few years back, right?"

"Yes, ma'am," I said, remembering the biannual event they did with high school girls. They had broken up the chapter into groups, depending on how many contestants there were, and each small group looked at it as fun competition to go against their peers to see who could raise the most money. If this was a down year and they didn't have to do that, those who would be excited to help us would take our contest to a whole different level.

"Why don't you and your committee meet us tomorrow night? I will round up some ladies who are willing to help, and we can go from there. Don't worry—when Betas come together, we can do anything. All is not lost. You all will raise a ton of money. Trust me," Soror Walker said, confident in her girls.

When I got off the phone and shared the news with my line sisters, we were all ecstatic. We didn't know to what degree they could help, but they were going to help. We had a map—we would meet them tomorrow to begin to execute it. We were going to help the King family. We were not going to give up.

Saturday evening had arrived, and all was great with the world for me. I was doing so great in school. The committee was thriving, working alongside the alumni chapter that was helping to show us how to put together a wonderful event. And on top of it all, I was in the car with Covin heading to his parents' house.

He grabbed my hand and put it on the stick shift as he led me to guide him into second and third gear. Chills went down my spine. He was awfully sexy and clearly

into me again. I knew now you couldn't smother a man—
that it was good to stay strong.

While I was being too quiet to function, he looked over
at me and said, "All right, beautiful, what's going on in
your pretty little head? Talk to me."

"I'm a little nervous about going to your parents' house.
You know, with meeting the senator and all his friends."

"Will you relax, girl? It's just a little birthday party for
me and my dad. It's no big deal."

"Oh, my gosh! It's your birthday? How didn't I know?
I should've gotten your dad something before I came!"

"Because you haven't been answering my calls. And
besides, my dad wouldn't want you to get him something
anyway. My parents are gonna love you."

We drove for about forty miles outside the city to a
beautiful, secluded, and gated community. It amazed me
how rich people liked to live on the outskirts, away from
everyone and everything.

"Hello, sir. It's good to have you home," the guard at
the gate said. "Your parents are throwing a big soiree."

"Thank you, Henry. This is my girl, Hailey. Hailey,
this is a man who takes care of me."

"She's lovely, young sir. You guys enjoy your night," he
said as the gate was lifted.

When we pulled up to the beautifully manicured, cir-
cular drive, there had to be four or five limos out front
and all kinds of high-priced cars on the street. I didn't
know how exactly I was going to master fitting in here
without being so fidgety. I was trying my best to control
my anxiety, but I think it was starting to take over.

"Okay, this is a lot," I said to Covin.

"All you have to do is be you. You can charm anyone with that smile of yours. How about this to calm you down," he said as he helped me out of the car and kissed me on the lips.

I had told myself he wasn't gonna get any anymore, but at that moment I wanted more, and I wanted to give it to him far away from the palace before us.

"Looking at this, no wonder you could have afforded all those beautiful campaign signs. Teddi and I could never have competed on your level. Covin, you live so modestly at school."

"Well, I just don't want money clouding anyone's view of me, is all. Besides, your handmade signs were really cute," he said facetiously.

"Yeah, yeah, yeah. Whatever," I said, playfully punching him in the face.

Before we could even make our way to the front entrance, a voice called out. "Son!" his mother said; she was in a lovely beaded gold dress. She looked disapprovingly at my gesture—she must have thought I was serious or for sure thought it was out of place.

Covin gave his mom a big, heartfelt hug, and the cold stare she gave me let me know I was not really welcome. The intuition I'd had to be apprehensive here had been dead-on. She'd already sized me up, and her nose was way up, because I didn't measure nowhere near up.

"Mom, I want to introduce you to someone. This is Hailey Grant."

"Son, I didn't know you were bringing someone with you," she said, wishing I was not there.

"Well, this is my birthday party."

"No, we're honoring you on your birthday—this is your dad's and my party for you. We paid for the meal, we invited the guests, and we want you to have a good time, our way, son. Trust me. So come on in and follow my lead. Your father and I have a surprise for you that is perfectly suited for you."

I so wanted to go vomit. I couldn't say, "Thanks for having me" or "I'm glad to be here," because that would be too fake. I was a little irritated. She too clearly let me know that I wasn't good enough for her son. Seeing the kind of stock he came from, I could tell I wasn't either.

"I need to go to the bathroom," I said to Covin under my breath.

"The ladies' room is down the hall, second door on your right," his mom said to me in a condescending tone.

There was so many people around—not that I wasn't comfortable with them, but I felt so out of place. I mean, Covin had me right—I could charm anyone anytime—but these were highfalutin, you-better-be-somebody-to-talk-to-me people, and I didn't have any of those credentials. Though my dad was an officer in the Navy, these were the kinds of people who were thankful for those who fought on the front line to protect them but could never befriend them.

Finally, I got myself together. When I came back out I realized deep down that I could do this. My sorority empowered me to be strong and feel confident in shaky surroundings. Covin wanted me here, and I wanted to be with him. I could prove to his parents, at least his mom, that I was a great girl. I looked in a couple rooms and couldn't spot him. Then I peeked in an open study to find him talking to his father. There was a young, semiattractive blond girl standing right beside him.

"Son, you have to be excited to see Mary. She came back from Harvard just to be here for this event."

"Covin, I hear you got accepted into Harvard Law School," she said as she gave him a big hug and a juicy kiss. Though it was on the cheek, it was a little seductive to me.

He'd been accepted to Harvard Law? At that moment, I hated I hadn't attempted to listen to all his messages. There was no way now that I could compete with Miss Blond America.

Mrs. Randall called from across the room, "Mary, dear, come and let me introduce you to some people. Covin, let me spare her for a second, son."

Mary smiled at Covin, and I was livid. She reached for his hand. I realized when he didn't reach for hers that maybe we had a chance. As she walked toward his mom, his dad's disgruntled face told me he wasn't pleased.

"You need to let me arrange to take home whomever you brought here," Covin's father said and then pointed at Mary. "What's standing over there is your future. You're at a HBCU for résumé credits and not to deal with folks beneath us."

Tears rolled down my cheeks. It broke my heart to hear Covin's father telling him, "That girl is not in your future plan."

# BEACONS

*C*ovin's dad went on and on about the poor choice he was making by wanting to be with me. I couldn't believe I was standing there quiet, still, numb, and taking in all the harsh words while the white chick was across the room with his mom, laughing and giggling like all was well with the world. Why was this happening?

But when his dad said, "She might be a good lay, son, but she's not going to get you into the White House," I was furious.

I just held my composure, walked into the room, and said, "You're right, sir. I'm glad I get to see the true colors of the senator I voted for re-election. You talk the good talk about caring for all the good people of Arkansas, but you're just an Uncle Tom."

"Son, are you going to let her talk to me like that?"

"I'm through talking, sir," Covin said, looking like he wanted to sock his dad.

I turned to walk out of the room, and Covin grabbed my hand. "Wait, Hailey. Don't go."

His mom came over and said, "What is going on here?"

Mary followed behind her and asked the same question. "Yeah, what's going on here? Covin, who is she?"

"This is my girlfriend. Mary, thanks for coming to show your support. Yes, I did get accepted into Harvard, Yale, the University of Arkansas, and many other Ivy League schools to practice law, but I haven't decided which one I'm going to attend yet. But I have decided that this girl right here—the one who hasn't thrown in the towel after what she just witnessed tonight—I want her in my life. Western Smith College may not be an Ivy League school, but leading the student body there, I am extremely proud. We come from a rich heritage that teaches us we can overcome racism and ignorance, even if it comes from our parents. Mom, you gotta want your son to be happy. You gotta want a woman who's gonna make me do better, like you always have. She has beauty on the outside, but there are a lot of brains to back that up. Don't judge a book by its cover or lack thereof. She's awesome."

Mary stepped up to Covin and said, "That's beautiful." She kissed him on the cheek. "I wanna find that. I'm happy for you guys." She walked out, nodding at me approvingly.

His dad quickly let us know Mary's thoughts were not shared. "Son, you're making a—"

"You know what, Dad? It's my life to live. I promise I'm gonna make you proud. Just trust my choices. No disrespect, but growing up, I've seen you and Mom around here, and y'all didn't have all that romance. I don't even know if y'all love each other. I want a little more than a certificate marriage."

"What's love got to do with it?" his mom said as she looked at me with harsh eyes.

"The same love you two have for me—your son. Let me have that real love all my life. You gotta take your hands off and let me go."

"You're saying you're in love? What are you two doing on campus? I hope no babies are on the way. If so, your life is going to be completely messed up! Where did I go wrong?" his mom yelled out before his parents exited the room and left us alone.

Frustrated, I sank into a nearby chair. Covin and I had finally found our way back to each other. We were ready for a healthy relationship. And now there was a big road-block that appeared to be a boulder we could not move.

"I'm so sorry for all this," he said to me. "I'll let her know she won't be a grandmom any time soon."

"I gotta go, Covin."

"No, you don't."

"Yes, I do. I'm gonna ruin your life. Your parents have planned so much for you. Your mom's right about love— we don't even know if we'll make it tomorrow as a couple. I don't want you to give up your future for what's uncertain with me."

"It doesn't matter about tomorrow. Right now I'm not gonna let go of my spot of hope. Say you don't care about me and I'll make sure you get home safely."

"You know I care," I said as my wet eyes got heavier.

"And now you know where I stand. Can we give that up? My folks will come around sooner or later," he said as he smiled. "We can't give up on us. Not when it feels this right."

He kissed me so softly and tenderly, and all felt right with the world. He'd let me know how strongly he cared. I felt good deciding we'd give us a real chance to be something.

"It's a glorious Saturday, Hailey! Today we are gonna rake in the money," Teddi said to me when she got off her cell phone.

We didn't even have to help the gents by ourselves. The alumni chapter had divided themselves into eight groups of three. Each group paired with a contestant and was holding different fund-raisers. One group had a bake sale. Two groups were doing a car wash. One was doing a barbecue. Another group held a fish fry. Three groups had a silent auction.

"All the events are going great. We just have to stop by, peek our head in for a bit, and give them some moral support," I said to Teddi.

"I'm so excited that the alumni sorors are really showing us if we stick around here, we can join their chapter. They don't just say they wanna work, Hailey. They are actually putting in work."

"Yeah, this is amazing," I said, very thankful that things were coming together.

We couldn't go to eight events in one day, particularly when most of them were between the hours of three to seven. So Teddi and I partnered up and went to the fish fry, which was being held in a local youth soccer complex. There were tons of cars and tons of families, and everybody was hungry. The event sold out.

The gent, whose name was Rashaun, came up to me and said, "Hailey, thank you for getting us help. I really needed some extra money for school next semester. And I do get forty percent of the funds, right?"

"As long as the money is going toward school for your books, tuition, and housing, yes, you get forty percent of the money—if you raise at least twelve hundred dollars. Keep working because, remember, you get sixty percent of anything raised over twelve hundred."

"Well, the only thing they have to do is put back the cost of buying the fish. Everything else was donated. I might be able to pay for two semesters."

Teddi and I stopped by the car wash, which was being held in the parking lot of the local Walmart. Not only were they making money on the car wash, but they had a lemonade stand, and people were giving plenty of donations.

"Hey, Hailey. I don't know how much these ladies have raised for me, but I'm sure it's enough," Stoney Creek, one of the male contestants, said to me. "My mom got laid off, and they didn't know how they were gonna keep me in school. This contest is a blessing. What can I do to thank these ladies for helping me out like they have?"

"Just stay in school, get good grades, and get a great job. I'm sure they wouldn't want you to pay them back."

"I have to do something. I mean, this gives me hope to do anything I want to, and I don't know how to thank them."

We jetted off again and went to our third event, the silent auction. It was an actual art auction. One of the chapter sorors was an artist and was previewing her new collection. She was selling paintings from previous years, and some of the bids were kinda scary.

Another gent, George, came over to me and said, "My dad got shot when I was eighteen. I had been living without my mom. She died from being strung out on drugs when I was a kid. If the pell grant hadn't paid my tuition, I don't know how I would have gotten here. Now I know I can make it."

Teddi's eyes started tearing up. I then realized she and this guy had a lot in common. They were both orphans, for lack of a better word, but they had both worked things out to come out okay. They both exchanged numbers and shook hands. We walked to the car, and I couldn't wait to clown her.

"Oooo, somebody is on the prowl for some new meat!"

"Whatever. We need to make sure we get all this money turned in tomorrow. That's the only thing I'm worried about. We were so focused on helping Ms. Mayzee's family that we rarely talk about the fact that these guys signed up and stayed with the program because they needed help themselves. This is really a good project, Hailey. Aren't you proud you're making a difference?"

"I'm proud *we're* making a difference, Teddi."

A hassle and a headache of putting on an event seem worth it when you were doing it for a justified cause. We were gonna be all right. Boy, did that feel good.

*    *    *

We were just beginning the May chapter meeting, and before we could start, our adviser walked in with some dignitaries. Oooos and ahhhs went throughout the room. When I turned around I, too, was shocked to see the National President standing at the back door. We all rose as protocol dictated. She was escorted to the front and conducted the official opening of the chapter meeting ceremony.

When she hit the gavel, and we sat down, she said, "Thank you all for welcoming me and allowing me to take part in this meeting. I came by because, as you know, Alpha chapter has been on probation, and I am pleased to tell you that the Panhellenic council for this university has not only decided to lift that ban, but that the chapter of the year is Beta Gamma Pi, Alpha chapter."

We all screamed across the room in amazement. This was so unbelievably untrue. The National President allowed us to bask in our excitement before she continued.

"Okay, ladies. Now, you guys know this award is given based on academics, evidence of displayed bonding, and public service. Basically, it boils down to which chapter is most effective on this campus, and this year it was you guys. You all brought in a line the right way through this tough economy, endured such natural disasters that no other group of women could make it through and came out on top. And on top of everything, you ladies overcame it all and shone with bright colors. And that's what Beta Gamma Pi is all about. We are light in the darkness. I'm not going to stay for your whole meeting, but I want to remind you to keep doing what you're doing. Keep on being the example. Keep on showing others the way. This chapter got off track a couple years back, and I didn't think Alpha chapter was going to make it, particularly when my daughter, Malloy, was in school. I'm about to go out of office, and I am so proud you guys have steered this chapter back in the right direction. Hats off to you all. Before I forget, I know about the young family you are all trying to help through your contest you have coming up in a few weeks. Please accept this five-hundred-dollar check from Grand Chapter to help them. I know the event will be pretty successful, and you will bless a lot of people."

The National President, along with our adviser, unveiled the Panhellenic trophy. It went alongside the many other awards the chapter had collected over its many years of existence. I was living history at that moment. Nothing could compare to me being a member of Beta Gamma Pi. We were truly the best, and that meant more than any trophy could certify.

As the National President exited the building, I gave a report, and lots of girls had questions. I knew every time I presented, there was drama, so I was pretty sure of what was coming my way. I dug my heels deep and prepared for the bashing to come.

"Why are we giving such a high percentage back to the gents and the family? Why aren't we keeping the majority of the funds for the chapter?" Sam asked.

"Because in the paperwork we gave to them it specified this way. We are trying to do good versus help ourselves," I explained, hoping the President would not forget what we signed up for.

"Well, if we have more money, we can help ourselves," Connie said. "I told them that amount was high."

"Too bad, Connie, because that's the way it's gonna be," Teddi said, speaking up as head of finances.

"The alumnae chapter helped raise that money for the participants. Sorors wanted to help the guys and us. And quit tripping, there's nothing in the documents we gave them that said they'd be disqualified if sorors helped them," I reminded.

People were going on and on and on about this money we had now raised. The bottom line looked to be about twenty thousand dollars, and of that we were projected to keep only four thousand. However, this was four thousand more than we'd had. I wasn't too hung up on the money part. The fight about finances ended in no agreement, and then the meeting was adjourned.

Afterward, Teddi came over to me and said, "You know we need to get the checks signed for the event."

"After that meeting, girl, I just need a break," I said, wanting a warm bubble bath.

Teddi grabbed my arm. "Girl, please! The President and Treasurer both have to sign, and are right over there. Let's take care of this. Then we'll have one thing done."

Heeding her point, Teddi and I went up to Sam. Before I could speak, Sam said, "I see there's a lot of discussion and a lot of rambling. Sorry we haven't been around your committee meetings too much lately, but we've been doing other projects for the chapter. Plus, I gotta make sure I graduate. I'm going to be honest—I don't feel comfortable giving this big percentage, but like y'all said, this is what we told them, so I'm signing off on the checks."

Because Teddi was in charge of finances for the committee, I gave her the checks to hold. As we walked to our dorm, she said, "I can't believe they're tripping over money. None of them were even on board for this event. They didn't help us raise a dime, ain't sold one ticket, yet they wanna trip about how we spend the money. Oh, please!"

"Don't let none of that stress you out or get you down. The checks are signed. We got what we need, and we know what we have to do to help people. Our committee is still treading along like the little engine that could. Despite all the negativity, hope still beacons."

## GOLDEN

"Come on, guys, this has got to be exciting," I said to my line sisters the day before the Mr. Beta Gamma Pi contest.

"Yeah, I'm just ready for it to be over with," Teddi said. "Are you gonna go meet Sam and get the rest of these checks signed off on?"

"Yeah. She's gonna meet me in a little while. Who all needs to be paid?"

Teddi handed me a sheet that was very well organized, listing the deejay, florists, and caterers who needed to be paid for their services.

Evan said, "You know, though, there's still been a lot of talk of what we're going to do with this money."

I was very aware that since we'd had the sorority meeting a week ago, sorors were still grumbling about the funds. It was interesting to me that when they'd thought the project wouldn't bring in a dime, they hadn't cared less if we had two legs to stand on. But now that they saw a large sum in the bank, almost every sister was weighing in on what we were giving out. I honestly thought we had squashed this issue and moved past it, but I heard the talk from everyone, even on my dates with Covin.

"Well, there's no need to worry," Quisa said. "They can do all the talking they want. We're the ones with the contestants' checks."

"That's true, that's true," Evan said. "Right, Hailey? Don't you have the checks?"

"No—wrong. Teddi has the checks. And they ain't going nowhere but in the contestants' hands and to Ms. Mayzee's family. I'll catch up with you guys later on. We can have dinner or something and go over everything one more time, but I think we're cool. I know this is the first time for this program, and nobody knows how it will turn out, but all the ladies in the house who bought tickets are going to go wild."

About thirty minutes later, I was walking into the sorority room. Sam called me out and said, "'Bout time you got here."

"I'm a little early, right?"

"No, I texted you, and told you I needed to meet you fifteen minutes ago because I have a job interview later."

Not caring for her attitude when I had been busy doing Beta business, I said, "Oh, well, I was meeting with my committee. Sorry I didn't get your message."

"Well, do you have to get me your report for tomorrow? I mean, like, what is it you need?"

"We just thought since the day's going to be hectic tomorrow that we should go ahead and get them signed off on."

"The checks? Yeah, I already signed those. I'm glad you brought those up because—"

"No, no, no. Not those checks. We need the ones for the other people helping us out tomorrow, like the caterers and deejay. It's all outlined here. I just thought if I could get those invoices to you now, you could get with the Treasurer, and they can be ready by tomorrow."

"Yeah, that's good thinking. Cool."

"Thanks. I don't need to hold you up, so I'll let you get to your interview."

"No, I actually need to talk to you," Sam said to me before I could get up to leave.

"Yeah, what's up?"

"I need you to hold those checks that I gave you for the contestants and that family."

"Sam, I don't know what you mean," I said, my eyes squinted. I was extremely confused and a little annoyed. We had already been there, done that. She'd signed the checks. What did she mean she wanted me to hold them?

She grunted like I had no right to question and then finally said, "My phone has been ringing off the hook with sorors. Everyone is still not one hundred percent sure that those boys should get the large sums you had me sign those checks for."

"Yeah, it was very clear in the package we gave them upfront."

"But the guys didn't raise all the money themselves—

they had the majority of the help from our sister chapter. If the guys needed money that bad, they should've hustled and raised it. But they didn't, so we're entitled to the money."

"How do you figure?" I asked her.

"Do you have the checks? Because I want them back now."

"No, I don't have them."

"Well, then, I'll get them tomorrow."

"I don't know if that's gonna happen. I've got to run this by my committee, and we'll call you."

Sam rolled her eyes and did not even try to understand where I was coming from; she acted like she'd given the last word, and that was it. She was acting like her words were the golden rule. This was a huge mess, and I had less than twenty-four hours to fix it.

When Sam left and slammed the door, I had steam shooting out of my ears! That was just how mad I was at that power-hungry, control-freak nutcase. Most of the sorors who were tripping over how much money we were giving away were graduating. I mean, my line sisters and I were the ones who had a few more years at Western Smith. If anybody cared about the bottom line, we should.

But we had made a decision, Sam had signed the checks, the rules had been set, and there was no way I felt comfortable not handing out the checks. My line sisters had just gotten through asking me if we were straight on the money before I had come to see her. I had no idea how they were gonna take this. As a leader, I was supposed to make them go for whatever the Chapter President wanted, right? Not necessarily—particularly when the Chapter President was being irrational and a tyrant.

As soon as I stepped outside our chapter room, my cell phone rang. Without hesitation, I shouted, "Yes!"

"What's up, babe? You okay?" Covin asked through the receiver. His voice instantly calmed me down. "I was just checking to see if I could meet my lady for a quick bite to eat. Do you have time? You should be done with your meeting, right?"

I really did feel bad because I'd really been putting him on the back burner, and this time it wasn't any part of a plan. I wanted to see my boo. He had gone from boyfriend to boo when he'd stood up for me with his folks. I wanted to spend time with him. But I was really focused to make sure this project went through how we'd planned. I wanted it to be smooth sailing from here on out, but now I was sitting in the middle of a perfect storm.

Sensing hesitancy in my voice, Covin said, "Just a real quick bite. It seems like my girl needs me." He didn't know how right he was.

"I'm already on campus. You wanna meet in the café?"

"Yeah. I'll be there in ten," he said to me.

I was there in five. And as soon as he came through the door, I thought maybe the cafeteria wasn't the best place for us to spend time alone with each other. He was the SGA President, and he wasn't being fake or phony when people came up to him and spoke. It was his job, his place to say hello and have small talk about this or that. It took him another ten minutes to make his way over to me.

"I'm sorry," he said. "I know you have a lot going on right now."

"It's fine," I said, knowing I did have bigger fish to fry, but I really dug seeing him care for the students.

He kissed me on the cheek, took my hand, and said, "Before we get something to eat, tell me what's wrong."

I took a deep breath and explained everything to him, from Sam's decision to the stress of the contest. I was in way over my head and needed to find some common ground somewhere.

When I finished my what-seemed-like-ten-minute speech, Covin shook his head and said, "You are in a pickle."

"How am I supposed to tell my girls and the people needing the money that I'm not giving out the checks when I myself know we promised to give them out? What in the world is right in this situation?"

I put my head on his shoulder and almost came to tears. He stroked my back and said, "Listen. It's tough being a leader. In your heart, though, is where the right answer lies. Don't let this defeat you, because when you're stressed, no good decisions come. Take a breather and meet with your crew. Y'all will work it out together."

Immediately, I texted my sands. Then Covin and I ate. It took less than twenty minutes for my line sisters to meet me in the café.

When I explained to them what had gone down, Teddi stood up and said, "Then I'm not showing up tomorrow."

Evan stood beside her and said, "Yeah, and when I tell the contestants they won't be getting any money, they won't be there either."

Quisa contributed to the mess by saying, "If they don't get their money, I'm not showing up tomorrow."

Millie, mainly quiet, spoke out and said, "I know I don't usually say much, but right is right, and wrong is wrong. I'm with them. No checks, no Millie."

My heart dropped like a bottle falls when released off a bridge. I really was caught between a rock and a hard place. I needed them to be at the contest with me, but I couldn't say I thought it was wrong for them to stand up for what they believed in.

"I don't know how I'm going to do this without you guys," I pleaded.

Teddi looked at me and said, "Well, you gotta figure out a way. Let's go, girls."

I should have been on top of the world right now. It was the night of the Mr. Beta Gamma Pi contest. We'd been planning for it for months, and my line sisters were in the house. So were the boys. So far everything seemed to be in place and going so well. The place was beautifully decorated, and a good vibe was passing through. Yet I had a knot in my stomach so large I could barely breathe. All of a sudden I heard a loud voice angrily yelling across the theater.

"Oh, no, she didn't! I cannot believe this!" Sam screamed.

I had been so shocked when my girls had told me they wouldn't be at the contest if the checks weren't passed out. I had asked them what we could do to solve this, because I knew there was no way I could pull this off without them. And with all the drama we'd gone through, people had to see the hard work we'd put in for this event. There was no way this contest wasn't happening. So I had agreed to something to get my line sisters there, and therein was the issue Sam was upset about.

"No, Cassidy, get off me! Where is she? Where is Hailey Grant?" Sam shouted at the top of her lungs as Cassidy gave us space.

"I'm right here," I said in a low voice as if I was hiding behind a curtain.

"We need to talk," she said as she pointed her finger in my face. "Why is Teddi out there giving out the checks I told you to hold?"

There was no way any of this could end well, but I was really irritated that Sam was acting like we had come to this decision out of the blue. After my committee had told me they wouldn't come, I had begged them to let me figure something out. I'd proposed we talk to Sam to find a solution. Surely, I'd thought Sam would be open to figuring out something when she learned my line sisters were not going to help with the event. However, we had called Sam four times from four different cell phones. And I wasn't saying she'd deliberately ignored it, but she had a track record this sororal year of deleting e-mails and staying out of things she didn't want to be a part of. When we couldn't get her, we'd talked to Cassidy, who was second in charge, and Cassidy had said she didn't have any issues with the money. We'd also talked to the Chapter Treasurer, and all the checks had cleared.

I hadn't done what I'd wanted to do with the checks—I'd done what I felt I had to do to get my line sisters to come help me pull off this event. I really felt that if Sam had had her way and hadn't given out her money tonight, she wasn't going to give what was owed to the boys, and that wasn't right.

Sam snarled at me like a grizzly bear. "Don't you hear

me talking to you? Why is she out there giving out the checks I told you to hold back?"

"We tried calling you—"

"Eh!" she said, putting her hand up to halt my words. "I don't wanna hear it. I gave the authority to hold the checks."

"Yeah, well, the checks were signed, and they weren't even in my possession."

"Oh, so she's doing it without your consent? Go outside and tell her you want them back then."

"I'm not going to do that."

"I just can't believe you," Sam said. "This is my chapter!"

I was so scared, but I wasn't going to back down. I started arguing with her. I guess we were causing the biggest scene ever because Cassidy came rushing in to try to grab Sam. Then my line sisters followed and tried pulling me back. Connie and her crew were in the same room as all of us behind the stage. They came in and watched.

The leader of our chapter said, "She's just gonna do what she wants to do and think I'm not going to have something to say about it!" And then she charged at me.

It was clear as day that she wanted to beat me down, but I held my ground. If it wasn't for everyone pulling us apart, who knows what would've happened.

"Come here, bi—" she called out.

I rushed out of the room when her sharp words tore through me like a steak knife. I felt our sisterhood was over when I exited the theater, and she called me a female dog. Alone, I sat in the stairwell and couldn't fight the tears.

*Lord,* I prayed, *there is no excuse as to why I don't talk to You much. Please forgive me. I do need Your help to figure this out. This is way out of hand.*

When I pulled myself together, I found the three guys who had been given checks and asked for them back. I found Cassidy and handed them to her. "Here."

"Hailey, are you okay?"

"No. She thinks I betrayed her when the only thing I was trying to do was make her proud she elected me chair for our first event."

"You can't worry about all that right now. You have to straighten up and pull it through to the end of the contest."

Despite all the drama, Sam and I were on the same stage hours later presenting the winners with their crowns. The packed audience had no clue that hours earlier we had been at odds. Teddi and Evan looked at me from the audience with their thumbs up. Connie was on the left of the stage winking, smiling like she was proud of me or something. I didn't know what all this was about. I knew it wasn't about the fact that we had put on a great event but was instead about me not backing away when my Chapter President had tried to jump me. I had brought in some money for the chapter. I'd helped some guys make their way easier. I was gonna be able to bless a family in a big way, yet I hated myself.

After the curtain went down, Sam eyed me hard and said, "This stuff between us is far from over."

As she stormed away, I thought about how life was supposed to be good. But I knew for me it was far from golden.

# PURPOSE

Shortly after the contest was over, Cassidy called an emergency meeting back at the sorority house.

"I'm not showing up to no meeting!" Sam yelled out.

Connie, Cassidy, and the other prophytes walked up to her and said, "You're coming whether you like it, love it, or none of the above. We all need to talk."

As I walked across campus with my line sisters, Teddi said, "Girl, you don't ever really go after anybody. People think you're so nice and sweet, but you finally let people know you're not a punk. You held your own."

"Yeah, you go, girl!" Evan said.

"We need to have her removed," Quisa uttered. As usual, Millie nodded along with no verbal input.

The four of them continued to converse about how wrong our Chapter President had been. While I appreci-ated their loyalty and their love for me, I wasn't one hundred percent right either. I had been given a direct order by someone elected to govern over our chapter, and I had disobeyed.

Contrary to what my line sisters felt about the situation, when—minutes later—we walked into the sorority room and Sam was telling people how I had given away checks she'd told me to hold, it was just a mess.

"Okay, everybody, settle down!" Cassidy shouted over the mixed voices. "This isn't a formal meeting. Our adviser's not here, but we definitely needed an emergency session. We can't even keep our in-house business in house because word is in the streets that we had serious fighting going on."

"Well, once everybody found out why I was upset with Hailey," Sam said when she took the floor, "people have been cool. I specifically told her to hold those checks."

"Yeah, but you've been showing your tail all semester. You tried to fight me, Cassidy, and now Hailey. You don't need to be our President!" Connie blurted out. "I talked to some of our line sisters, and everybody is not with you. We are thinking about going to the Regional Coordinator and getting you removed."

The Treasurer said, "Wait a minute. You can't be mad at just Sam. A letter just came in the mail about the alumni chapter supporting Hailey Grant's candidacy for Second Vice President at the upcoming convention. She didn't even tell any of us she was running. No wonder she was working so close with them and trying to get them cool with her. If anyone needs to be ousted, it should be Hailey."

I could hear Teddi and Evan getting ready to battle for

me. But I touched both of them and stood up myself and said, "Look, I didn't tell anybody about running for a position because I never agreed to run. I'll talk to my mom and see what that's all about—if they even sent out false information about me. However, I doubt it, because an alumnae chapter knows you can only campaign when you have been slated. They would not break rules. You must have misread the letter anyway, because when you're running from the floor, you can't send correspondence. I want to see this so-called letter."

"Um, well, are you denying it?"

"Yes, I'm denying that I accepted. And after everything that happened tonight, I don't deserve to be anybody's national officer. I can't speak for Sam—"

"You daggone right you can't," Sam said, cutting me off.

"But the reason I became a Beta was to make a difference by helping this chapter and our community. Though my decision was partially wrong, I felt it was partially right because I wanted to help Ms. Mayzee's family, those boys, and our chapter."

"She shouldn't have talked to you the way she did. And you had to protect yourself!" Connie called out.

"That's right," Teddi said.

"Again, I can only look at myself in the mirror, and at this point I don't like what I see. I didn't join this chapter to protect myself against my sister. So you don't have to overthrow Sam. That's not in my character. I gave the checks back to Cassidy, so you can do with them however you like. I'm done." And I walked away to head to my room.

I wondered how could I have let things get so off track. And as much as it hurt leaving my sisters, things were irreparably broken. Walking out had been the right thing to do. I had to punish myself in some fashion. I was wrong even though I was right.

"Oooo, so Covin is really handsome," my sister, Hayden, said to me while we were on a double date with our men.

I couldn't believe that in just a few months she would be married. And although Covin and I weren't walking down the aisle, I knew he was a big part of my world. I had come to understand that all college relationships didn't last forever, but looking at Hayden and Creed, I hoped for the best and promised to hang on as long as we could.

"Hailey, come with me to the ladies' room," my sister begged. As soon as we got into the restroom, she tugged me. "Okay, I just said your man is fine, and I barely got a reaction from you. What is going on with you? I heard the contest turned out nice."

"Yeah, and you also heard about the drama with Sam."

"Yeah, but I told you beforehand that going into this sorority thing I wasn't perfect as an undergraduate myself. Life is about making mistakes and learning from them. It's okay to punish yourself, but it's like you're locking yourself up for good and throwing away the key. I think we should all leave here and go over to that King event together."

"No," I said to my sister; I felt she was trying to push me. "I don't wanna be around the Betas."

"Hailey, they're doing the right thing. They may have

questioned the amount at first, but it is a good thing they decided to give five thousand dollars to the King family. You're a big part of making that happen, and you need to be there to see your dream come true."

When we got back to the table, it was like Covin had heard our whole conversation because he said, "I need to go to the Kings' house. SGA's helping with the presentation, and I need you to be by my side."

"I told you already," I said to him, "and I said to Hayden that I didn't wanna go."

"Come on, babe. I need you with me. I never removed you from my cabinet as director of community relations. So, technically, it's your job. You've been slack on it, so you shouldn't be giving me any lip. We won't stay long. Come on," Covin pleaded.

"Okay, fine," I said, giving in to both pressures.

Hayden and Creed rode with us. When we got to the Kings' house, tons of people were there, including two camera crews. Covin insisted I head up front with him, but I said, "This spot right here is fine. Now, I agreed to come, and that should be enough. Please don't make me go up there."

When he got to the podium, my uncle came out of the house with Ms. King and the kids.

"Why is Uncle Webb here?" I said to Hayden.

She squeezed my arm and said, "Just wait. It gets even better."

Next out of the house came Covin's parents. The senator approached the crowd and said, "When our son told us what was going on with this family, I went to my fellow state senators and congressmen and collectively went to work. We are thankful for Mayzee King's actions in saving so many kids, including my son."

"And my niece," President Webb said, standing behind them.

Sen. Randall said, "As well as all the other children she risked her life to save. We do want to honor her memory today by presenting three ten-thousand-dollar scholarships that will be put away for her children to attend college."

My eyes just watered up. This was fabulous beyond my dreams. I knew our event couldn't do everything, but it had ignited others to help.

"We also reached out to some local businessmen, and the floor and roof of this house is going to be fixed. This place is going to receive its own makeover, thanks to the great citizens of this state. Be proud of your community, help out when you have the chance, and embrace your neighbor. This is the beginning of a fellowship, and the progress is going to be appreciated to the maximum degree." The senator stepped away, and applause was given from anyone who had hands.

Covin followed behind his father and said, "Now I would like to introduce the President of Beta Gamma Pi for another presentation."

As Sam approached the mic, I swallowed hard.

All she said was, "I had a presentation to make, but—"

Time out. Had she said "had"? See, I knew something was up. This was more drama from the chapter, but in public. Did she plan for the chapter to keep the money after all? I had thought Hayden had talked to someone and knew the check was finally gonna be presented to Ms. King. Ugh! I was so angry.

Then my foot got stuffed in my mouth when Sam shocked me and announced, "But I realize I am not the one who should make this presentation. I am aware that Hailey Grant is among us today. She's the one who spearheaded this whole effort and had the right heart to want to do bigger and better things for this family. Hailey, I can't do this without you. Could you please come forward?"

The spotlight was on me. Everyone turned to face me to see if I would accept her offer. I was no mean person, nor did I hold grudges against people, but we'd had one heck of an ordeal. Placing my feelings to the side, I picked up my feet and slowly but surely made my way to the front of the crowd.

As I walked toward the mic, Sam said, "So many of us get things wrong. Sometimes we want things to be about us and what we say. Hailey Grant taught me you gotta have self-reflection. I'm better. Our sorority is better because she cares so much." I got to the podium, and she whispered in my ear, "Forgive me."

I smiled and wiped my face. We presented Ms. King with a symbolic check for her daughter's memory. It felt great to put aside some crucial differences and bring out the good for others in need. I walked away from the podium with my head held high and the attitude of an improved, faith-filled young woman.

As soon as the event died down, Covin's parents approached me. I wanted to walk the other way. However, I knew I couldn't be rude.

"Looks like you make a lot of people look in the mirror. Sorry we misjudged you. Sorry we didn't open our eyes to know our son can make great choices. He spent months trying to make a difference for this family, and that's awesome," his dad said, giving me another surprise of the day.

His mother touched my back and said, "Because of how you wanna take care of someone else, I know you will be able to take care of yourself and my son."

"I told you she was all that, Mom!" Covin said from behind me before he gave me a big hug.

To think I hadn't wanted to come. I'd wanted to stay away. I was glad I'd let go and followed the leading of others. This was one of the proudest points in my life. I was a part of really making a difference for a family who had lost everything. On the up and up, it seemed like Sam and I would be able to work things out. And, by just being me, I had ended up showing Covin's parents I was worthy enough for their son. Somehow, in my spirit, I could feel Ms. Mayzee smiling down at me from heaven. Turmoil was worth it sometimes, particularly when good came out of the madness.

"I can't believe my mom talked me into going to this conference," I said out of frustration to Covin.

I was speaking to my boyfriend on the phone. I was in Atlanta, and he was back in Arkansas. The Beta Gamma Pi conference was one my line sisters had been anticipating for a while. It was our first one, for goodness' sake. My line sisters were in the room next door, and I was sharing a room with my mom and my sister. At this point, everyone was at the opening session, and I just wasn't feeling it, so I had called my guy to complain.

"Listen, you're there now. You pledged Beta Gamma Pi to learn more about the organization and make a difference. At a National Convention, I can only assume it helps to fine-tune you," he said like a guy who loved networking.

"Yeah, I miss you, and it's devastating to know you're going to be going off to law school soon."

"Actually, I decided to go to the University of Arkansas. I wanna stay around here. My state needs me, and, hopefully, someone else does, too."

"Not going to an Ivy League school is suicide for your political career."

"Please. Knowing I want to be a state politician and going to the largest school in Arkansas is an asset to me. Plus, I want to be around a special young lady. So, it's cool. About you, though—I know you might not be feeling the whole sorority thing for whatever reason, but you're there. You need to make the most of it. If you wanna get something out of it, you at least have to put in the time."

He was absolutely right, and he made a lot of sense. I immediately got dressed and texted Teddi to see what side of the large auditorium they were sitting on. I guessed I was gonna make the best of it.

"What made you change your mind?" Teddi asked me when I sat beside her.

"Covin told me to take it all in."

"Well, I know I told you before, but, again, I was way wrong," she said.

"Wrong about what?" I asked, needing my memory to be refreshed.

"I said he wasn't a good choice for you. He's actually

exactly what you need." I reached over and gave her a big hug. "I still should be SGA President though."

I just laughed. "He's leaving, so you can try next year."

"You're right," she said and kissed me on the cheek.

There was a break between sessions, and my mom and her Chapter President came over to me. My mom pinched my cheek, and that meant she wanted something. I wasn't into meeting more important Betas. I knew it was important to personally know our leaders, but it was also important to enjoy my sands at our first convention.

"People from different regions have been coming up to us asking who our candidate is for Second Vice President. Nobody else has another choice. Say you'll do it," my mom said to me.

I turned around to try to walk back up to my room, but Teddi was standing right there with the rest of my line sisters. They were nodding on my behalf. Even Sam, Cassidy, and the other prophytes surrounded us.

Sam walked up to me and said, "You better represent and make us proud, even if somebody else decides to run with you from the floor. We're gonna win this. You need to lead us. I lost my way, and you helped me."

Evan came up to me and whispered, "Because of your love and leadership, I finally had the courage to walk away from an abusive relationship. You care like no one I know. You must run."

My sister took me by the hand and said, "I got robbed four years back. I had rumors keep me from becoming elected. Run and win for me."

I loved my sister. She had always been my hero. I kissed her and walked by my mom. I nodded, ready to accept the challenge of being nominated for a national office in my beloved BGP. I guess I'd given much more good than I knew to receive such support.

Soror Walker took to the mic and said, "Madame National President, for the office of National Second Vice President, I nominate Miss Hailey Grant from Alpha chapter."

Soror Murray said, "Thank you for that nomination. Do I have any others for this office? Going once, going twice, hearing none . . ."

A collegiate soror wearing a skirt that looked five sizes too small, had five different colors of bad weaves, and long gold nails that made it almost impossible to hold the mic said, "Miss President, I'm Soror Gina Bell. I'd like to nominate myself for the position."

The room erupted. I knew the image of this girl was not what we needed for the organization. However, I didn't want another fight. I was headed to withdraw my name.

Seeing me head toward Soror Walker, Hayden got in my way. "Hailey, I know you. Don't back out. Your experience will be different from mine. You know you're the leader we need. Give it your all. If you don't try, you get nothing."

We hugged. The National President slated both of us. I had to give a speech in an hour. Locking myself away from everyone to concentrate, I struggled on what I'd say.

Sixty minutes later, I was listening as my opponent took the microphone and said, "Look at me—I'm a college student who knows who I am. We college kids aren't alumnae sorors yet. We're young, and we need not to act old. I can help keep the sorority young. Vote me, Gina

Bell, and when I win, you can ring it at my par-tay. We shouldn't take this so seriously. Laugh, y'all." The room was still. "Well, just vote for me then."

I wasn't here to down anyone else, but this girl had no clue. My sorority was serious to me, and I needed to give a speech my man would be proud of.

Standing on a platform in front of the crowd of Betas, I took a deep breath and spoke from my heart. "As I look out into this full audience at my lovely sisters adorned in purple and turquoise, I come humbly seeking the office of Second Vice President. I'd like to be elected because I believe you get what you give. I want to give my whole heart, body, mind, and soul to this organization. And if I can serve on the highest level to spearhead policy ideas, enforce the rules and laws, keep alive the rich tradition of our founders, and inspire Betas as I hold the office, I know I'll give back much in return. We Betas are powerful women. Though we have different opinions and different talents, we all have a collective goal: we all want more for our community, more for our sorority, and more for ourselves. As your Second Vice President— unlike my opponent—I'd take this very seriously. I'd make sure each and every soror is reminded that united we stand and divided we fall. There is a way to work out our differences. We are sisters, leaders, educators, and Christians who give. When I was pinned as a part of the sorority, much was given to me. Much was given to us all. Now it's time for us all to give back, give all, give more, give big, and give strong. Elect me, Hailey Grant, your National Second Vice President, and together let's give all we can for our beloved BGP. We are worthy of nothing less. Thank you."

The auditorium went wild. Immediately, the voting began, and when it was announced that I was Second Vice President, Hayden squeezed my hand.

"I wanted this so bad four years ago. But God knew what He was doing. He gave office to the one who sees the worth in every individual, the one who wants to get better, the one who doesn't think she's worthy when she clearly is. You are the essence of Beta Gamma Pi. I'm proud of you, little sis. The collegiates are in really good hands, and so is Alpha chapter because I know you're gonna lead with purpose."

# Beta Gamma Pi, Book 5:
## Get What You Give

## Stephanie Perry Moore

### ABOUT THIS GUIDE

The following questions are intended to
enhance your group's reading of
Beta Gamma Pi: GET WHAT YOU GIVE
by Stephanie Perry Moore.

# DISCUSSION QUESTIONS

1. Hailey Grant is the campaign manager for her best friend, but she doesn't think she's the best candidate. Do you think it was right for Hailey to support Teddi's candidacy? What are ways you can be there or be a friend to someone even when you're not supporting everything he or she does?

2. When the fire breaks out, Hailey goes back to try to get Teddi's important objects. Why do you think it was important for Hailey to help her friend by risking her own life? What are things you do to show others you truly care for them?

3. Covin Randall has Hailey's interest. When she knows her best friend may have a problem with this, was Hailey right to keep it a secret? What are positive ways to deal with tough issues you know won't please someone you care about?

4. Hailey isn't sure that Beta Gamma Pi is for her. Do you think it was a smart idea for Hailey to check out the other sororities? Why is it important to do your homework and check out organizations and groups before you try to join them?

5. When Hailey finds out Teddi has not made the line for Beta Gamma Pi, she goes to bat for her friend.

Do you think Teddi would have done the same if the shoe were on the other foot?

6. After Hailey is chosen to become chairperson, she receives tons of resistance. Do you think she handled being a chairperson correctly? When you are the leader, how can you get others to follow, especially when you know they are envious of your position?

7. Covin wants to take their relationship to the next level, but Hailey wants to see other people. Though she wasn't ready to go further in the relationship, should she have pulled so far away that it led her into the arms of another? What are some good dating do's and don'ts?

8. The sorority is trying to raise money to help others in the community. Do you think helping others was the driving force behind Hailey getting her own life together? What good does one get from helping someone else?

9. Later, before the big charity event, Hailey and the Chapter President have a heated exchange. Do you think fighting resolves anything? What are positive ways that conflict can be worked through?

10. What points did you get from the speech Hailey gives to the delegates when she runs for national office? How are you striving daily to give more than you take?

Can't get enough of sorority life?
Turn the page for more of Stephanie Perry Moore's
Beta Gamma Pi series.
Available now, wherever books are sold!

# BRIGHT

"So you think it's okay if somebody whacks you upside the head, calls you all kinds of names, beats your behind, and who knows whatever else, Hayden Grant? I've even heard of cases where sororities make pledges perform some kind of sexual act," my mom Shirley voiced in anger, as my caramel face turned pale.

"Mom! I can't believe you would go there with me."

"What, Hayden? Don't be shocked. I know how bad you want to be a Beta and I know you might lose your mind to get what you want. Plus, you're about to be a sophomore in college, at a predominately African-American school. I know there are several nice-looking young men around grabbing your attention. Something made your grades slip last semester. I think you're still pure, but we need to talk about sex."

"I can't talk about this with my mom. I just can't," I said, shyly turning my head and twirling my mid-length do.

"Better she talk about it with you," my sister, younger by four years, popped into my room and said.

"Hailey, have you been standing there the whole time? Quit being nosy," my mom scolded and shooed her away.

"We were talking about being a Beta, Mom. We weren't talking about me and sex," I quickly reminded her.

"Well, I'm not done. I think any young lady that makes smart choices will do that across the board. If you make wise decisions, particularly when the alternative is giving it up to some boy who the next day probably won't know you exist. You could wind up pregnant or with some disease. Isn't it better to stay away from all that? Someone who's strong enough to resist temptation and stands for what God says is right, will not want to be a part of some group that thinks the only way you can get in is to participate in some form of illegal activity that the organization doesn't even tolerate," she said, getting louder and louder with each sentence.

"Okay Mom, I get it! You don't have to go on and on and on about it," I said to her, extremely frustrated.

I didn't want to go there with her, but it seemed to me like she needed to get her groove on. My dad Harry was away at war. He's an officer in the Navy and his girl had too much idle time on her hands. So much so that she was all up in my business.

My mom knew I wanted to be a member of Beta Gamma Pi ever since she pledged the organization's alumnae chapter when I was in the fifth grade. After she became a member, I remember many nights during my childhood when she was away with the service-oriented organization, working in the community by taking food to the poor, being there for the elderly, and helping the uneducated gain knowledge. Even though part of me resented not having all of her time, it just fueled me, excited me, and made me want to strive to become a member one day. My mom had wanted to pledge as an undergraduate when she was in college, but due to females tripping, she didn't. I had a deep longing to obtain that goal for her.

My mom came over and got right in my face. "Let me just tell you this really quickly. I desperately want you to be a Beta. But if you participate in any of that foolishness and anything happens, I don't want you calling me. I don't want you thinking that I can help save the line. None of that. Do you understand? I'm telling you now, I don't support hazing and in the end it only divides. Be a leader on that campus, Hayden Grant."

She went on to explain, for the fiftieth time, the legitimate steps to becoming a Beta. First, there was rush, where an informational session is held and the members of the organization explain all about what they stand for and what they do. They also distribute application packets to the prospective candidates, which need to be turned in by a certain date. After the packets are returned and reviewed by the members of the organization, then comes the interview. But not everyone will get one. After the interview, if you receive enough votes from the sisters of Beta Gamma Pi, then you become a part of the pledge line. After handing in the money for the pledge fee, a Pi induction ceremony is held. There are five Gem ceremonies and an Eagle weekend hosted by the alumnae chapter, which pledges must attend. Next there is an intense week of studying the history of the sorority and a major exam is given before the candidates are ready to cross over and become sisters of Beta Gamma Pi.

"You participate in any other activity and it's hazing. Got it?"

I nodded. Of course I heard her, but I couldn't say what I would and wouldn't do once pressure from the Betas was applied. I didn't want to be ostracized and considered paper because I wouldn't participate in a few little uncomfortable things. I mean how bad could hazing really be, right?

There are certain rules that go along with the way many people think is the best way to pledge. First, pledging on the collegiate level carries more weight than pledging in an alumnae chapter. I thought this was crazy. However, the rationale is that collegiate chapters really make members do things *way* over and above what the standard rules call for. Also, many believe that if you don't go through the collegiate process then you are not a real pledge, only a *paper* one. And let's face it, if you have the chance, who wants to be called paper? Definitely not me.

Then there is the legacy rule. In some sororities if your mother is a member and you have the qualifications, then there is no vote necessary. You automatically become a member. But, with Beta Gamma Pi, that isn't the case. Since my mom didn't pledge on the collegiate level, their preferred methods, I knew I was going to have to pay for what she didn't go through. I was ready for it, because I knew if I made line I could legitimize my mom's place in the sorority.

"I'm gonna make you proud, Mom. You don't have to worry," I said, stroking her verbally and psychologically.

"Honey, all you need to do is concentrate on your grades and be the best Hayden you know how to be. If the Betas don't want you, it's their loss. You can always pledge the way I did," she said in a sweet tone, so I'd keep my hope. But I wasn't having it.

My mom wasn't all excited about the way she pledged. She knew the stigma attached to alumnae pledge methods. Though I knew deep in my heart that being put through an intense pledge process didn't make one a better member, if I had the opportunity to get all my props, I had to do it. Why would she think I wouldn't want all the respect?

My mother continued, "Now see, I can tell by your face you think pledging on the alumnae level is not kosher."

"Well, it was your dream to pledge undergrad," I quickly reminded her.

"Yeah, but just because that didn't work out doesn't mean that I would go back and trade my experience for anything. I was so connected with the ladies on my line. And quite honestly it was absolutely the best timing. God knew what He was doing. And Hayden, for you to have the outcome that He wants for your life, you have to ignore what others say and just focus on what is right. You know how to be a strong person, but a strong leader knows that God's way is golden. So seek Him and figure out what He wants for you. Plus, I truly now believe pledging on an alumnae level is the best way to join the organization," she said with her worried eyes locked on mine.

I smiled, feeling she believed those last words. I hugged her to let her know though I wanted a different experience, I was going to be okay. Then I was off to college. Western Smith University, here I come. It was time to get my sophomore year started.

We hugged, and then I was off. It was time to get my sophomore year started.

From *The Way We Roll*

## BECOMING

If I see one more Beta Gamma Pi girl looking down at me because I'm not sporting any of them pitiful letters, I might just kick her tail. Yes, I'm here at their convention, but I am not Greek. I'm not here like other wannabes; I'm here because I have to be.

My mom, Dr. Monica Jenkins Murray, is their National President, and that makes me sick. I can't believe my time with my mom has taken a backseat to the sorority. For real, when it came to my mom doing sorority business versus my mom being a mom, I came last every time. Yeah, she said all the sorority stuff was for the good of the community and one day I'd understand her sacrifice, but when she didn't make any of my piano recitals or, parent-teacher conferences, I started to detest the group she loved.

After my parents divorced and my older brother moved out with my dad, it was just my mom and me. Though we lived in the same house, we were worlds apart. Basically I felt Beta Gamma Pi took everything away from me. I was at the National Convention only because some of the ladies on the executive board were more of a mom to me than my own mother. The First Vice President, Deborah Day, who lived in California, begged me to come support their endeavors. Because she was always there when I needed someone to talk to, I came. Plus, the VIP rooms in the hotel were stocked with alcohol. With no one around to supervise, I was feeling nice.

"You're all smiles. I guess you just finished kissing the National President's butt, huh?" I said to a girl coming out of my mom's presidential suite.

"I'm sorry, do I know you?" the girl said, squinting, trying to figure out who I was.

"You're so full of it," I said, calling her out as I stumbled, trying to get my key to work on the door. "You know who I am. You're just trying to get on my good side to raise your stock with her."

The girl persisted. "I'm sorry, I'm not trying to offend you, but you really do look familiar. Do you need some help with that?"

I snatched my hand away. "I don't need your help."

"What's going on out here?" The door flung open, and my mom came out in the hallway.

"I was, uh, trying to get in the room." I fell back a little.

"Girl, you are so embarrassing me. Get your drunk behind in here now," my mom said sternly. Then she sweetly spoke to the other girl. "Hayden, come in, please."

"Wasn't she just leaving?" I said. I was so confused. My mom went over to this Hayden girl and just started explaining my behavior, like she needed to apologize to some college girl about how I was acting. Why couldn't my mom apologize to me that I had to put up with a brownnoser?

"Come here, Malloy, I want to introduce you guys," my mom said. I reluctantly walked over to them. "Hayden Grant, this is my daughter Malloy Murray. Malloy, Hayden is the Chapter President of Beta Gamma Pi on your campus."

"See, I thought I knew you." The girl smiled, and she reached to shake my hand. "I'm going to be a junior. I knew I'd seen you around school, but I didn't know this was your mom."

"Yeah, sure you didn't know this was my mom," I said sarcastically while keeping my arms glued to my sides.

My mom huffed, "Lord, you don't have to be rude."

"Then don't force me to talk to someone I don't want to talk to, and don't apologize for how I'm feeling. I have a right to be angry, okay, Mom? I don't want to embarrass you anymore, so please get this girl out of my face. I don't care what school she goes to. Unlike both of you, I don't think Beta Gamma Pi is God's gift to the world."

"Hayden, I'm so sorry about this again. Let's just keep this between us. My daughter doesn't usually drink. She'll be much more herself when you guys get back to school. Let's just say I do look forward to working more closely with your chapter, particularly when Malloy makes line."

"Yes, ma'am," Hayden said, really getting on my nerves. She could not get out of the suite fast enough for me. Of course, after she left, my mom looked at me like she was disappointed. Shucks, I was the one rightfully upset. The alcohol just allowed me to finally let out how I felt.

"Mom, don't go making no promises to that girl about me being on line. I'm in school to get an education, not to pledge. Plus, their last line was crazy. They haze up there. You want me to have something to do with that? You're the National President. You're supposed to be against any form of hazing. I'm telling you it was all around school that they put a girl from the last line in the hospital."

She looked at me and rolled her eyes. I believed what I was saying. Some of those girls would do anything to wear Greek letters. Not me.

Changing her tone, she said, "Sweetheart, if you're a part of it, they won't do anything like that. I don't have to worry about anybody doing anything you don't want, as tough as you are. Just promise me you'll take this into consideration. This is one of my hopes for you, Malloy. Being a part of this sisterhood can be so fulfilling. You don't even have a best friend, for crying out loud."

"Yeah, for crying out loud, one of your biggest dreams for me is to be in a sorority. Not to fall in love with a man and stay married forever—like you couldn't. Not to graduate from college with honors and get a great job or doctorate—like you did. Instead, you're praying your child gets into a sorority. I might have had a couple drinks, but it's clear to me that's the thing you want most for me." I plopped down on the couch, picked up the remote, clicked on the television, and put the volume on high. "Don't hold your breath on me becoming a Beta. Sweet dreams, Mommy."

She went into her part of the suite and slammed the door. I knew I had disappointed her. However, as much as she had disappointed me in my life, we weren't anywhere close to being even.

"Mikey," I said the next morning as I came out of my side of the large executive suite I was sharing with my family and saw my brother watching the sports channel with his friend.

"Hey, sis," he said, squinting his eyes as he looked at my outfit.

I hadn't realized my silk gown was open, and the little nightie I wore was revealing much more than my brother wanted his friend to see.

"Cover up, girl. Dang," Mikey said.

"Not on account of me," his friend said with a smirk.

The guy was so fine. I could see the outline of his chiseled chest through the T-shirt he wore. When I looked harder I knew exactly who he was. It was Kade Rollins, the starting linebacker for the University of Southeastern Arkansas.

Mikey was a defensive back on the same team. He wasn't that great, but he'd started. On the contrary, this Rollins guy was great. I remembered the sports writers wondering why he didn't go pro last year. Kade was staying for his senior year to graduate and make his stock go even higher. He was predicted to go in the first round of the draft.

Kade's dark mocha eyes were so into me. I was actually loving the glare. It made me feel sexy. Mikey was furious. I turned around and went back into my room as Mikey followed.

"What's up with that? Why are you going to come out and be all disrespectful like that? Fix your clothes."

## BARRIER

"Alyx Cruz in the house. I'm a Beta Gamma Pi girl—get out the way! Alyx Cruz in the house. I'm a Beta Gamma Pi girl—I work it all day!" I chanted as I swayed my Latina hips from left to right at the National Convention's collegiate party for my beloved sorority, Beta Gamma Pi.

I wasn't trying to be funny or anything, but as a Mexican in a black sorority, it was not easy. I had it going on. The looks I got from men told me they wanted to get with me, and the looks I got from girls told me they wanted to be me, or they hated me because they weren't. It wasn't my fault that I didn't have kinky hair and that mine flowed more like a white girl's (though, truth be told, some days I wished mine was kinky—maybe then I'd fit in with everyone). Though they couldn't see it, I felt like a true sister from my core. But most Betas felt a Spanish girl shouldn't be in a predominantly African American sorority. If they'd take time to get to know me they'd see I was down for the same things they were. That's why I joined Beta Gamma Pi.

However, if another one of my sorors looked at me like they wanted to snatch my letters off my chest, they were gonna be in for war—a real fight. I hated that I'd had to transfer to a new school. I'd finally gotten people to like me for me back in Texas, but because I'd partied just a little too much—okay, well, not just a little too much, a lot too much—my grades had suffered. And I'd put my scholarship in jeopardy. It was a minority scholarship, for which you had to maintain a 3.0 grade point average. I'd had to find another school that would take me with my 2.6 GPA, but I'd wished I could fix my mistakes. I hoped I wouldn't squander another great opportunity.

Now I was gonna have to start all over again winning friends at Western Smith College, my Tio Pablo's alma mater. My uncle helped my mom and me come to the United States from Mexico when I was three. He'd died when I was six, and it had been me and my mom ever since. My mom kept his framed degree in our house to inspire me to do more. So I applied to Western Smith and thankfully got enough financial aid to attend.

I couldn't get an education any other way. I had an opportunity, and I couldn't be crazy with it. I had to make sure I seized the chance. Here I was in America living the dream, and I had been about to waste all that. But now at Western Smith, I had a second chance.

But I couldn't focus on any of that, particularly when my favorite song came on. "Hey, get 'em up, get 'em up!" I started shouting as I turned, swiveled, sashayed, and bumped into that girl Malloy I'd met an hour before.

"I am so sorry," I stuttered, taken back at seeing Malloy with about fifteen of her buddies all staring hard at me like I'd stolen their men or something.

"Oh, no, you're fine. It's perfect anyway. I was just telling my chapter sorors here about you," Malloy said in an overly sweet tone.

All these girls were from the Alpha chapter at Western Smith, where my sorority was founded. For some reason the girls in this chapter really thought they were better than everybody else. I could tell by the way they looked at me that they wished I'd go crawl under a rock. But I was on my way to their campus, and I already had my letters, so they needed to get over themselves. I looked at them, my hand on my hip and my eyes fully awake, like, "What . . . what you gon' do?"

"*Okayyy,* let's have some hugs and some love," Malloy said as she pushed me toward them.

The hugs I got from some of the girls made me want to throw up. They were so fake with it. When I got to the last few, I didn't even move to hug them. I wasn't a pledge. They could respect me or keep stepping. A few of the girls turned their noses up at me and walked off. I didn't care, because the sorors I pledged with would always be there for me when I needed sisterhood.

Then Malloy touched my shoulder and whispered, "Wait, please let me introduce you. Please."

Something in her gesture got to me. I didn't know her from Adam, but she was genuine. I really appreciated her wanting to make the awkwardness dissolve.

"These are my line sisters Torian and Loni"—neither girl standing next to her said hello—"our Chapter President, Hayden Grant; Bea, our First Vice President, and Sharon." Those three didn't even put up our sign, which was customary when you met a new soror.

"Now y'all, for real, you're being rude," Malloy scolded as she turned her back to me and tried to get her chapter sorors straight.

She didn't have to go defending me. I could hold my own. Shoot, they didn't want me in their chapter. Well, too doggone bad. I was coming, and what were they going to do about it?

But then, as I saw them continuously staring, I realized they were seriously feeling threatened. They didn't know me or my heart. I had to make them feel comfortable and let them know I wasn't trying to mess up their game. So I said, "Hey, I know it's tough accepting an outsider into your fold, but in my soul let me say I feel like family. I mean, I am your soror. I know a lot of Betas who aren't really excited about Spanish girls, but trust me, I don't want the spotlight, and my letters didn't come easy—I was hazed. I just want us to be cool, all right?"

Bea smiled and stuck out her hand for me to dap. When the other girls smiled as well—I guess now they knew I wasn't paper—we were cool.

"To me, more importantly than how I pledged is why I pledged," I continued sincerely. "I plan to make a difference in the community and I love this organization. Just give me a chance."

All the girls finally gave me a real embrace. I didn't know where we'd go from here, but I was excited to find out.

# From *Got It Going On*

## BENEVOLENT

*Y*eah, I know I got it going on, and even with all the eyes rolling my way, I'm not gonna feel bad about that. My dark, almond-toned skin is glazed to perfection. My 5'7" body is slim in all the right places. My sassy short do moves the men. I know how to work it. Every guy at this Student Government Association back-to-school party is checking me out, including the fine, commanding SGA President, Al Dutch.

Al Dutch—yes, he wants everyone to use his whole name all the time, saying he plans to run for political office one day and we need to remember him. Al is a lady's man; he looks, walks, and talks like money! You know the type. The one who's confident and cocky and always has a sure smile plastered on his or her face, with a no-worry, got-much-loot look in his or her eyes. Al's that

232 Stephanie Perry Moore

type. His skin glows like he has slept on the best satin sheets and used the finest body oils all his life. All the men wanna be him. All the girls wanna be with him—including me. It was game time, and I was flirting hard.

Western Smith is your typical historically black college with even more bells and whistles. We are rich in history in our great state of Arkansas. We have everything at our disposal—a good football team, excellent academics, amazing Greek life, and great cultural campus events. Western Smith even has a first-rate band—which is the place where I fit most.

I was a drum major my sophomore year. Now that I'm a junior, I've switched gears and decided to try something different. Now I'm captain of the dance team. One would think my life is perfect, but my reputation isn't the best. Though I don't care what people think or say about me, I know I want to make the line of Beta Gamma Pi. Three years ago when I first came to college, I was at a probate show where the sisters were stepping, and I remember all the excited oohs and ahhs they received from the crowd. It was then that I knew I really wanted to be a Beta. Plus, their sorors in my hometown of Natchez, Mississippi, helped get me through my high school years and because of their scholarship, I was able to attend Western Smith.

After meeting some Betas in middle school, I had researched the sorority. I found newspaper clippings about the five founders, and I'd even taken a tour of the National Headquarters about thirty miles from campus. The more I looked into what the Betas were all about—leadership, sisterhood, education, Christianity, and public service—I knew they were the sorority for me. The whole God thing wasn't really my thing, but I knew to be a Beta, I had to either clean up my act and hope they would vote me in or cancel that dream altogether.

# HAVEN'T HAD ENOUGH? CHECK OUT THESE GREAT SERIES FROM DAFINA BOOKS!

## DRAMA HIGH

by L. Divine

Follow the adventures of a young sistah who's learning that life in the hood is nothing compared to life in high school.

## BOY SHOPPING

by Nia Stephens

An exciting "you pick the ending" series that lets the reader pick Mr. Right.

## DEL RIO BAY

by Paula Chase

A wickedly funny series that explores friendship, betrayal, and how far some people will go for popularity.

## PERRY SKKY JR.

by Stephanie Perry Moore

An inspirational series that follows the adventures of a high school football star as he balances faith and the temptations of teen life.

# GREAT BOOKS,
# GREAT SAVINGS!

### When You Visit Our Website:
## www.kensingtonbooks.com
### You Can Save Money Off The Retail Price
### Of Any Book You Purchase!

- **All Your Favorite Kensington Authors**
- **New Releases & Timeless Classics**
- **Overnight Shipping Available**
- **eBooks Available For Many Titles**
- **All Major Credit Cards Accepted**

### Visit Us Today To Start Saving!
## www.kensingtonbooks.com

All Orders Are Subject To Availability.
Shipping and Handling Charges Apply.
Offers and Prices Subject To Change Without Notice.